EVERYTHING

To: Catherine.

Alan D. Howard.

8-11-2017.

ALSO BY A.D. HOWARD

Walk Thru People – another powerful novel
of an unbelievable event – *that might just happen!*

EVERYTHING CHANGES!

by

A.D. Howard

BP
Bookaholics Publishing, Lincolnshire. 2017.

BP
Published by Bookaholics Publishing
19, Carters Garth Close, Grainthorpe, Louth,
Lincolnshire LN11 7HT

Everything Changes!
A.D. Howard

ISBN: 978-1-910693-99-5

Cover designed by Pageset Limited, High Wycombe, Buckinghamshire.
Printed in Great Britain by Print2Demand Ltd, Hastings, East Sussex.

This book is dedicated to Ann

Contents

CHAPTER 1

THE INCIDENT

The sleek, black limousine silently drew up outside the main entrance of the office block. The doorman scuttled down the steps, crossed the pavement and opened the car's passenger door. A tall man in his mid-forties emerged. He was dressed in a neat light-grey suit, topped off by a full head of chestnut coloured hair.

"Good morning, Minister," the doorman said. "Welcome to Spatial Tower."

"Good morning," the Minister replied and strode off towards the building.

On the opposite side of the car, his bodyguard exited from the other passenger door. The car rocked slightly as the anti-gravity drive adjusted to the change of weight, now that the passengers had alighted. He looked over the top of the car to see his charge climbing the steps to the building. "I wish he wouldn't do that," he said under his breath, "he's supposed to wait for me. He'll regret it one day."

They met up in the extensive atrium. Daylight flooded in from the large windows that surrounded the space, creating a natural feel to it. It wasn't crowded, although there were a large number of people milling about, each with a communicator held up to the ear of their choice.

The duo headed for the left-hand staircase. They'd been here often and knew the way to the conference room, which was located on the first floor. The staircase was empty, apart from one man about halfway up. The majority of people chose to use the lifts, but the Minister always liked to take some exercise before sitting in a conference room. It calmed his mind.

As they passed the man, he was only given a cursory glance, as he was involved in a conversation on his communicator. When the Minister had climbed two steps above him, the man swivelled round and pushed the side of his rectangular belt buckle. The Minister immediately fell flat on his face. The man then returned to his original orientation. The bodyguard dropped to his knees.

"Sir, Sir, are you all right?" he asked, thinking that he had tripped. When he didn't receive an answer, he felt his neck for a pulse. Nothing. The Minister was dead. "Help! Help!" the bodyguard shouted.

"I'll have to leave it there. There appears to have been some kind of accident." He switched off the communicator and slid it into the pouch on the front of his navy jacket. Then he turned to the bodyguard. "What's happened?" he asked.

"The Minister has died," was the reply. "Call for help while I tend to him."

The man did as he was asked and within thirty seconds the staircase was swarming with security officers. The man wasn't worried about leaving fingerprints behind, as he didn't have any and because he wasn't trying to leave the building, he was just thought to be an innocent bystander.

It was only a few moments later when the ambulance arrived. This was a usual occurrence, as most life-threatening conditions were picked up during routine body scans and treated accordingly. The ambulance crew were sufficiently medically trained and able to prescribe the majority of drugs. They quickly came to the same conclusion as the bodyguard. The Minister was dead. The sense of urgency subsided somewhat, as the main task now was to remove the body.

It was a legal requirement that all sudden and unexplained deaths were to have a post mortem; no longer did that mean cutting the body to ascertain the cause of death. Now, a 3-D body scanner would scan the body and highlight any problems it found. After the scan was completed, it took the electronics a few minutes to process the information and arrive at a conclusion.

The scan of the body was displayed on a screen and a printed read-out of the conclusions was provided. In the early days of the scanners, old-style post mortems were carried out, to confirm the conclusions reached. This practice didn't last long, as the physical examination only tended to confirm the scanner's conclusion. So the scanner's results were always accepted and in the case of the Minister, the display highlighted his heart in red as the seat of the problem. The accompanying printed read-out stated the situation in complex medical terms. But, in everyday language, it was as if his heart had been switched off, causing him to die instantly.

As he had been a Government Minister, the matter was looked into more closely than was normal. His doctor's records were studied meticulously, but there wasn't anything that rung any alarm bells. The Minister's death was recorded as "Sudden onset heart failure. Cause or causes unknown".

CHAPTER 2

WELCOME TO NIVARNA 7

On the majority of planets the space-port is the busiest location, as it was on Nivarna 7, which is one of the twelve planets terra-formed to make them suitable for agricultural use. They were required to feed Earth's burgeoning population, along with the planetary settlements that had been established.

As the atmosphere had to be kept free of pollutants, propulsion-driven transport craft were not allowed to land on any of the Nivarna planets. They remained in orbit and anti-grav drive craft from the surface would collect empty payload containers. These would be returned to the planet and replaced with containers filled with the correct crops. On return to the orbiting craft, these containers would be locked into place, readying the transport for the remainder of its journey.

There was room to carry a few passengers, if required, although these facilities weren't used very often. This journey, however, had brought a passenger; a planetary drifter was to visit Nivarna 7. News of this traveller quickly spread among the residents. They'd heard of such drifters before, but never had the opportunity to actually meet one. A few of the older farmers truly believed that accounts of planetary drifters were, in fact, legends and stories originating from the early days of space exploration. But now they would have the opportunity to meet a drifter "in the flesh". They felt sure that he would be far more interesting than the usual visitors that came to the planet: managers, scientists and technicians, being the regular fare.

All those involved in the successful reloading of the transport craft headed for the spaceport entrance, with the drifter bringing up the rear. He decided that following them was the best way to be guided to the nearest bar, a place where he could guarantee people would gather together. He had learned one thing during his many travels; that the bar was the best place to size up a planet and its residents.

As they approached the entrance two officials stepped out,

ready to check those who desired entry. Although they were scanned, as the law required, the residents were quickly ushered through. The drifter deserved a more detailed inspection. To start with they ran the scanner over his left forearm and to their relief, a green light was displayed. (The scanner had read the information stored on a chip in his arm. It had been embedded there following his birth in line with the practice for all newborns.) The officials were too settled in their ways and didn't want to deal with any problems. Now there were a few more checks to complete.

The drifter carried a small black bag that was slung over his right shoulder. The contents needed to be checked, after all this is an agricultural planet, so alien species possibly carrying unknown diseases needed to be kept out. Fortunately, the bag only continued a few personal items. Following a scan of his clothing, he was waved through. He was now allowed access to Nivarna 7. The drifter didn't worry about all the checks that he was subjected to, he'd been through the process many times before.

The officials turned and watched the drifter walk slowly away from them. "Imagine the work involved checking him out if we still used passports, as they did centuries ago," one of them said.

"All the items that would have to be checked: identity, exit and entry visas and all the rest. It almost fries the brain just thinking about it," his companion replied. (Passports were now curiosity items on display in museum cabinets.)

The drifter soon entered the main area of the port. He needed a bed for the night, as he didn't fancy sleeping under the stars on an unknown planet. After all, he had the odour of a new planet to adjust to. He'd needed to adjust many times in the past, as each planet had its own distinctive smell; even among planets that served similar functions.

It didn't take much effort to locate the bar. He entered a rectangular room fitted out with tables and chairs, along with a cluster of comfortable chairs, for those who wanted to discuss things in a more relaxed setting. The bar itself was the largest feature in the room. It ran for almost the full length of one of the room's longest sides. The wall opposite the bar was fitted with large panes of glass, providing a panoramic view of the countryside. Many a solitary drinker would look out at the view, while lost in their thoughts.

As he entered an unfamiliar bar he usually found the occupants would turn around to check him out. After all, they weren't that used to strangers casually walking into their bar. But that didn't happen this time. A few heads briefly turned in his direction and then turned back to continue their conversations. He had been around people for long enough to have learned behavioural characteristics. There was obviously something that was troubling these people and he was astute enough to know that he would eventually learn what the problem was.

The drifter sat down on a stool by the bar and waited for the barman to take his order. He asked for a beer, which he found to be a good judge of a planet. It was usually the case that good beer equated to a good planet. There were important items to be concluded at this point. The first would be pretty straight forward, but the second may well turn out to be more difficult. When the barman returned with his beer he asked him if he would mind telling him the date and the current time. He reached into his bag for his Pocket Personal Computer. He reset the clock with Nivarna 7's date and time, although deep in the electronics another clock was running. The read-out for this clock had to be requested, by following specific commands. This one was set to Earth date and time.

He took a long satisfying drink of his beer and then wiped his mouth on the sleeve of his jacket. He called the barman over. "Out of all the people in this room, which one is mostly likely to provide me with a bed for the night?" he asked.

The barman scanned the room's occupants. "Let me think about it," he replied. "I'll go and see the customers at the end of the bar, then I'll come back."

The drifter watched him serve the customers, engage in a brief conversation with them and then walk almost the full length of the bar back to him. "I would think that walking the length of the bar so often as you do would keep you pretty fit?" the drifter stated.

"It certainly helps," the barman replied. "By the way, those last two customers I served asked me about you. They seemed quite interested, but didn't want to approach you themselves."

"I hope you were complimentary," the drifter said, hopefully.

"At the moment, I've no reason not to be. Anyway, returning to your need to find a bed for the night. There are three distinct possibilities, based on the information that I've picked up over time."

As the barman pointed these men out, the drifter followed his directions in the large mirror mounted on the wall behind the bar. He didn't want to warn them that he was heading in their direction. He had one more question for the barman. "Are there any women on this planet?"

"Most of the farmers have their wives with them, but they don't usually visit the bar during the week. Although at the weekend, especially Saturday night, this place gets quite lively."

"Thanks, very interesting," the drifter replied. "I didn't think that a planet only populated by men would function very well. Anyway, I think it's time to enter the fray and approach the first candidate that could possibly help me out."

After approaching two farmers he hadn't made any headway. They both had their wives at home and were used to having the place to themselves. At least the meeting with them was pleasant and cordial. One more person to try, otherwise he may well be sleeping under the stars. He walked towards the farmer who was sitting alone at a table in the corner of the room. As he drew closer to him, he noticed that he appeared somewhat older than the other farmers at the bar.

"May I join you?" the drifter asked.

"Help yourself."

"Thank you. It's possible that you can help me out."

"I don't see how I can help you."

"I'm looking for some kind person who can offer me a bed, as I don't have anywhere to sleep tonight. I'm quite happy to work in payment." They sat there in silence for a good few minutes.

The drifter had learnt over the years that it wasn't a good idea to rush people into making a decision, especially if you had asked for assistance.

Time passed. Then the old farmer lifted his head and spent what seemed like an eternity staring into the drifter's eyes. Finally he spoke. "I've been widowed for over seven years and it's about time to have someone sharing the house again. So, in answer to your request..."

Here it comes, thought the drifter.

"...I feel that my offering you a bed, for the foreseeable future, will serve us both well."

"Thank you so much," the drifter replied and then asked a question. "As we going to be living under the same roof, it would help if I knew what to call you."

"My name is Santos, Santos Memphis. That's the first time I've spoken my name in a long time."

The drifter noticed a flicker of a smile on the old man's wrinkled face.

"If you wish to abbreviate it, that's okay with me."

"Let's keep it simple – Santos – if that's all right with you."

"That's fine. Now what do I call you?"

"My name is Javan – just Javan," the drifter replied. "And if you wish to abbreviate it, go ahead, although most people tend to use it as it is."

"That seems an acceptable arrangement. You call me Santos and I'll call you Javan. I'm glad we've got that out of the way," said the farmer.

"After that strenuous brainwork, I think we both deserve another drink. Shall I get you a beer? The one I had earlier was rather tasty."

Santos nodded his head and Javan headed for the bar.

When the barman saw the look on Javan's face, as he approached the bar, he felt that his guidance had borne fruit. "I presume that you have been able to conclude your accommodation arrangements?"

"Yes, indeed. Thank you for your help. Could I get you a drink?"

“That’s very kind of you,” the barman said, “but I don’t drink. I know this sounds strange, seeing that I serve drinks all day, but actually it’s a protection. I don’t want to become another alcoholic barman – there’s enough of them already.”

“That sound reasonable,” Javan said in response, “but who knows, I may well find another way to thank you in the future.”

Javan carried the beers back to the table and sat down. The new friends were soon deeply engaged in conversation, discussing their individual histories, life experiences and their individual hopes and dreams. Anyone looking at them would think that they’d been friends for years. The bar’s other occupants were astounded. They’d never seen Santos talk with another person for that length of time before, now it was happening right before their eyes. The wives would have to be told about this development, when the menfolk had finished their drinks and ventured home.

CHAPTER 3

WHERE THE HELL DID THAT COME FROM?

Nivarna 3 was about to experience a problem, a planet-wide problem.

As part of the crop rotation cycle, that all the Nivarna planets followed, Nivarna 3 was growing root vegetables. The farms around the planet were growing every variety of root vegetable known to mankind. A whole planet following the same cycle prevented any form of pest to take hold, even though such pests are supposed to be eradicated before the seeds were dispatched.

The majority of farmers on the Nivarna planets enjoyed sitting outside their farmhouses, watching their particular sun setting and the appearance of their various moons.

Nairn Whittle was sitting in his rocking chair, a mug of beer in his hand, daydreaming as he luxuriated in the evening sun. A sudden movement in his turnip crop caught his attention. No longer dozing, he was wide awake now, convinced that he'd imagined the shape that had briefly appeared in the crop. Now he paid close attention. He didn't have to wait long. This time he was sure – he'd seen a rabbit in his crop. That was the last thing he, or anyone else, wanted.

Nairn called his wife and asked her to join him for a moment.

"What do you want?" she said, "I'm busy preparing dinner!"

He told her what he'd seen.

"You've been drinking too much, it wouldn't be the first time that you've seen things."

"Look, I've barely touched my beer. Just look over there for a few moments. That's where I saw it."

So they watched and waited, enjoying the evening sun and then, as if on cue, a pair of rabbits scuttled into view and had the nerve to nibble on a few plants, before they hopped away. "Believe me now?"

"I think you should inform the authorities as quickly as possible. After all, there may only be a few now, but they breed like... er – rabbits, don't they?"

There followed much toing and froing over a variety of communication networks, culminating in the quarantining of Nivarna 3 and the dispatch from Earth of a specialist team of exterminators. News of the rabbit infestation quickly spread to the other Nivarna planets and those growing crops that could be decimated by rabbits, or any similar creature, were especially vigilant.

Even using one of Earth's fastest ships, it still took nine days for the extermination team to arrive. A couple of empty transport pods were used to bring the personnel and their equipment down to the surface. They set up their equipment in the largest of the space port's meeting rooms and the secondary one was used as sleeping quarters. The team was made up of eight men and two women who formed the extermination team and six scientists, two men and four women, who performed all the necessary tests required.

Following the day's activities, it was late in the evening when everything was set up, checked and ready. It was decided that the operation proper would begin the following morning, when everybody had had a good night's rest, followed by breakfast and the obligatory coffee. Then they would be ready for the day's procedures to begin.

The first item on the agenda was to catch some live specimens, to be able to establish their genetic code, blood groups etc. Catching these animals was down to the field agents. Armed with humane traps they set off, placing the traps in the widest possible variety of locations. To get about and cover the large distances involved, the agents used mini one-man transports. The nearest equivalent, from before the development of anti-grav drive systems, would be the helicopter. But these single-person transport units didn't have to use rotors, to obtain lift, as they used to do.

Each of the humane traps emitted an encoded radio signal, to aid their location and recovery. Despite the integral use of technology, it still took most of the day to place all of the traps. By the time the final agent returned, the sun was rapidly approaching the horizon. All they could do now was wait. When the trap had tripped it sent out a message to indicate its status. This signal was monitored at the base and an agent could be dispatched to collect the trap. If another creature had been captured, as was occasionally the case, the creature was released, the agents' fingers being kept well out of the way, just in case. Then the trap was re-set and replaced.

By the middle of the fourth day, they had collected enough specimens for the scientific tests to commence. The agents were able to collect all the traps, bringing them back to the base. When they weren't needed any longer, they could be sent for cleaning and sterilization, ready for re-use.

All of the scientists began their work. When it was completed the pests could be eradicated but before this could happen, they had to establish the origin of this non-native species, along with their estimated reproduction rate and the best method for their eradication.

They worked late into the night, consuming large amounts of coffee, along with some special tablets, to assist their staying awake and alert. The first breakthrough came just after two o'clock in the morning. To ensure that a mistake hadn't been made, as the result was so unexpected, she asked her fellow geneticist to check and re-do all the tests again. He came back just over an hour later and confirmed the original findings. Before they revealed their findings, the biological team announced that they'd reached their conclusions. It was decided that they would all have a break for an hour and grab whatever rest they could manage.

No one actually managed an hour of rest and by the time forty-five minutes had elapsed, they all gathered together once again. As the genetic team were the first to reach their conclusions, they would start the revelatory process. Their tests indicated that all of the rabbits were clones; there wasn't any genetic variation between the animals. They'd completed every test they could, always arriving back at the same conclusion. The remainder of the team were astounded by this discovery, never having come across such a situation before.

"Our findings fit in with yours," the leader of the biological team announced. Once the group had quietened down, she continued with her findings. "We were in a similar situation to our colleagues and re-did our tests a number of times, only to prove that there wasn't a mistake. These rabbits are all sterile, therefore there isn't a problem of their numbers swelling.

Despite the unique situation that they found themselves in, the animals that were causing problems needed to be eradicated. When that had been completed, there would be time to try and establish their origin and purpose.

A communication from a farmer, not long after sundown, changed the whole tenor of their task. He'd been out walking in one of his fields, checking the condition of his crop and came across a number of dead rabbits.

"I've gathered them up and will be with you in about twenty minutes," he said. The scientific teams prepared for his arrival and could foresee a long night ahead.

The farmer duly arrived and handed over the sack containing the corpses. They thanked him and advised him to scrub his hands with an antibacterial wash, then an ancillary member of the team accompanied him to the bar. The scientists were all wearing protective gloves, just in case there was a transmittable disease involved. Once the investigations started, it didn't take long to establish the reason for the creatures' sudden demise. Having the samples they had from their previous investigations helped tremendously and speeded up their arrival at a conclusion.

The planet's natural insect population had provided the solution to the issue. A tiny wasp had taken an interest in this new creature and decided that it was the ideal host for its eggs, which in turn had caused a toxic reaction in the rabbit's blood and led to its death from a sepsis of the blood. So this,tiny insect that none of the team had ever seen before, was inadvertently doing their job for them and using natural means to eradicate the problem.

When the team's report was received on Earth, it created a buzz and was added to the list of unexplained events on the Nivarna planets. As to the question of the infestations, origins and purpose, that went unanswered - for now.

CHAPTER 4

ANNIVERSARY

They exited the bar through a door in the end wall, that opened onto a path that would lead them to the transport pods. Walking this route presented Javan with his first opportunity to fill his lungs with Nivarna 7 air. He noticed some odours that he didn't recognise, although he knew that he'd soon become accustomed to them. He tried to take a good look at his new home, although his view was somewhat limited for the moment.

"I've never seen pods like that before," Javan said.

"Just wait until you see what they can do," Santos replied. "This one will be all right."

"Are they not allocated on an individual basis?"

"No," Santos answered. "I'll show you why, when we're seated inside." Santos pressed a button on the side of the bodywork and the whole transparent canopy lifted up, allowing them to climb inside and settle into the two individual, cushioned seats. Once settled, Santos depressed a button on the small control panel and the canopy closed over them.

"Well, what do you think?" Santos asked.

"Very nice, apart from the fact that we're facing the wrong way."

"Just watch this," Santos said, as he pushed another button. The entire passenger capsule turned through 180 degrees and then locked itself into its new location. Javan could now see where they would be heading. The ground seemed to be covered with a lattice of thin metal strips about four inches wide.

"Are they the rails that we travel on?"

"Not in the conventional way. They provide the electronic signals required to operate and direct the pod."

"What system is used to determine whether the 'driver' is allowed to use the system?"

"A simple, foolproof method of confirmation was decided on. I place my two thumbs on the pad and the internal circuitry compares my prints with those that are held on record. Are you ready to get underway? I just need to key in my destination code, then confirm and away we go."

The pod began to ease forward and only began to gather speed once it had traversed the mass of guidance strips. Javan was impressed with the acceleration; although he wasn't forced back into his seat, he could definitely feel it.

"How fast do you think we're going?"

"I don't know. There isn't a speed indication on the control panel. Maybe that's a good thing."

Javan put the speed of the pod to the back of his mind and took the opportunity to study the landscape. He soon came to the conclusion that there was a mixture between familiar Earth plants and many alien species that he'd never seen before. 'I presume that they were part of the planet's indigenous flora, from before the terra-forming,' he thought to himself.

Javan put his landscape investigation to one side for the moment. He saw something in the distance that he'd been waiting for. The metal strip that guided the pod came to a junction. The main strip carried straight on, but another strip crossed it at right-angles, effectively forming a cross. He was interested to see how the pod dealt with the situation. He need not have concerned himself. The pod didn't alter its speed, as it approached the crossroads and sailed straight across as if it wasn't there. That's answered that question Javan said to himself and then started to ask Santos about various aspects of the landscape and the distance they would cover.

At this point in time, Javan had no idea how far the pod had travelled and when he saw another junction approaching he didn't pay any attention to it. As this junction approached, the pod reacted differently. It began to slow down and at the junction it turned left and then began to increase its speed again.

"Almost there, now," Santos announced. "I'm glad that I don't have to drive a car over this journey every time."

"That's one thing I never did. I've only been in the newer electronically directed ones."

"You don't know what you're missing." Santos replied. "There are places on Earth you can go to experience traditional driving. If you ever get the chance, it's an exciting experience."

Javan looked through the front of the pod and saw that there was a rooftop just visible above the horizon. He realised the speed the pod was travelling when he saw how quickly they were approaching the building.

The pod began to slow and then stopped outside the front of the farmhouse. Santos opened the canopy and they got out, Javan carrying his shoulder bag that contained his possessions.

"Welcome to The Homestead," Santos said. "The name was my wife's choice. Come on in and I'll show you round."

Javan was allocated what had always been classed as the spare room and as such, had mostly been set aside for storage. A number of boxes and other items had to be removed before Javan could move in. It was also referred to as the front room, as it looked out over the verandah and was beside the main entrance to the house.

"You won't need to sit outside to watch the sun set, you can sit and watch it through your window. I think you'll really enjoy the experience, or you can sit out on the verandah and think things through."

"I'll use the time each evening to update my diary," Javan said.

"Do you use paper and pen? It's surprising how many people do, especially the wives," replied Santos.

"No, that would be a bit too bulky for me, as I like to travel light. I keep my diary on my PPC."

"Out here among the stars, we tend to call it a pad. It's a name that's developed over time. You can tell whether someone's from Earth that way."

"That's worthy of note," Javan replied. "I'll keep that in mind."

"You get yourself settled in and then come through to the kitchen. Just follow your nose. I'll rustle up something for us to eat."

Santos left Javan sitting on his bed and headed for the kitchen. It didn't take Javan long to organise his few possessions. He had to reset his small bedside alarm clock, to Nivarna 7 time and then set the alarm to a time he thought would be suitable. He then made sure where all the amenities were. It was important to get this into his memory, just in case he needed to get up during the night.

An appetizing smell emanated from the kitchen and Javan realised how hungry he was, not having eaten since the morning.

“It seemed really strange setting two places on the table again. It’s been years since I needed to,” said Santos. “When my wife died, it took at least six months before I got out of the habit. Anyway, that’s enough of that. Come and sit down, the food’s almost ready.”

While Javan waited he looked around the kitchen. His eyes settled on a 3-D laser print of an attractive middle-aged woman. He realised that this was the only picture he’d seen anywhere in the house. He drew in his breath and asked, “Is that a picture of your wife?”

“Yes, that’s my Jenny and even though it’s been a number of years since she died, I still miss her very much, sometimes more than others.”

'I know that feeling so well,' Javan said to himself.

During the meal Javan had a question that he had wanted to ask ever since he had entered the bar that afternoon. 'Now’s as good a time as any,' he thought. “When I first entered the bar this afternoon, I couldn’t help noticing the different groups around the tables, all involved in a discussion that they were engrossed in. Do you happen to know what the subject was?”

“Sadly, I do,” Santos replied. “Over the last year or so, there have been a number of unexplained occurrences spread across the Nivarna planets, slowly increasing in their frequency and intensity. Just last week, there was the worst incident to have happened so far.” Santos paused for a moment and took a couple of large swigs from his mug of coffee. Then he continued. “It happened on Nivarna 6. A farmer, Nicholas Chernon, was ploughing one of his fields in preparation for the sowing of his next crop. As all the fields on the Nivarna planets are much larger than normal, we all use non-standard equipment; the ploughs are controlled by a tractor unit, that is computer controlled using GPS signals transmitted from the geostationary weather control system satellites. A human controller rides in the tractor unit and has overall control. But when you are hauling three extra wide plough units behind you, it's much easier and more efficient to allow the computer to control the system. Everything that takes place is recorded in the onboard log of the tractor unit. If it wasn't for that, we wouldn't have ever been able to establish what had happened. Over half of the field had been ploughed, when a red warning light flashed on the control panel, indicating a problem on plough unit three. The rig was stopped immediately, the engine switched off and the key removed. He climbed down from the cab and walked back to unit three. Nothing appeared to be wrong. All of the connections and linkages were checked, all was as it should be. So he got down on his knees to see if any of the blades had become jammed or clogged. While he was doing this, the engine started and the whole unit shot forward, then it stopped and the engine switched off. You can imagine the state poor farmer Chernon was in and he could have laid there for hours, were it not for the fact that the field was alongside a pod track and a passenger in a passing pod raised the alarm."

Javan sat there mesmerised, he hadn't heard of any of this before. There must be a very effective news blackout, he thought. Santos returned to the kitchen table, after rinsing his coffee mug out.

"An incident of this magnitude necessitates investigation and so a delegation arrived from Earth, charged with establishing what had taken place and trying to place blame wherever they could. The farmer was the prime candidate, even though he was the victim. The investigators studied the tractor unit's log every way they could, but they were unable to find fault with the farmer's actions. He did everything correctly and, anyway, he wasn't anywhere near the tractor unit when it suddenly came to life again, if only for a few seconds. But that was long enough to cause a fatality."

"That's incredible!" Javan said as he collected the plates and cutlery together and took them to the sink. As he started to wash them up, he said, "And you say that there's been other unexplained incidents, all across the Nivarna planets?"

"Definitely. Almost too many to mention. Some very trivial, but annoying and others of a much greater intensity."

"Back on Earth, nothing about this has crept into the media at all."

"Just think what would happen if it did," Santos said. "The panic that would set in, if the population thought its food supplies were going to be disrupted. I'm sure that you know what people are like. How long would it be before the rioting and looting started?"

"So thinking about it that way, it's easy to see why the government have ensured that this news stays secret," Javan replied.

When the kitchen had been tidied up, Javan announced that he was going to sit out on the verandah and watch the sun set.

"I'll join you, when I've watched the news telecast," Santos replied.

It was a temperate evening, with a slight breeze. Javan sat down on one of the two rocking chairs provided on the verandah and removed his pad from his jacket's inner pocket. He selected a particular file and almost instantaneously a young woman's face appeared on the screen. Three dates in her life were listed under the image, Birth, Marriage and Death. Javan selected the next page, which had Earth date and time displayed on it and confirmed what he already knew: today would have been his anniversary, had Ann lived. He started reminiscing, reliving that terrible day five years ago.

Javan had taken the day off work, to tidy up the flat and prepare a special anniversary dinner. After all, this was their first anniversary and he wanted to do all he could to make it a special occasion. The only thing he was unable to organise was the weather. It was a drizzly, overcast March day. Although this didn't really matter, they were young and in love, just wanting to be together.

As he wasn't there when the accident occurred, he only learnt what had taken place from the police and finally saw it for himself some time later when he plucked up courage to watch the CCTV footage. He was on his own as he watched the images unfold in front of him. He took a sharp intake of breath when he saw Ann emerge from the legal office where she worked, chatting away with one of her friends. The conditions had made the stone steps at the building entrance slippery.

When he saw Ann stumble he gripped the arms of his chair and then saw her fall backwards, hitting the back of her head on the steps. She was rushed to hospital, but it was too late. She'd damaged her brain stem and died instantaneously. Javan switched off the footage at this point and kept it for future use. After all, these were the last images he had of his true love and had transferred the images to his pad. Even after all of these years, he still couldn't bring himself to view them again.

At this point Santos arrived. "Are you all right?" he asked, noticing the tears on Javan's cheeks.

"Just memories," he replied and switched off his pad then slipped it into his jacket pocket. "Anything interesting in the news cast?" he asked, changing the subject.

"Just the usual politicians and experts waffling about nothing of any importance. I don't know why I bother watching it every night. I suppose I hope something important will crop up eventually. Anyway, fancy a glass of beer, it'll help you to sleep?"

"That would be most welcome," Javan said.

They sat there in silence, sipping their drinks and watching the sun slowly sink towards the horizon, only to be followed by the majestic sight of the two moons rising into the night sky. The larger of the two was similar to Earth's only it was a deep creamy colour. The second moon was about one third of the size and was a powder blue colour. The light reflected from the two moons blended together to produce an ice-blue colour which provided spectacular shadows.

"You get used to the colour after a while," Santos said, that being one of the final pieces of conversation before they decided to call it a day and retire to bed.

CHAPTER 5

TIME WILL TELL

As summer slowly drifted into autumn, there was a steady increase in the number of complaints about interference on a variety of data transmission platforms. An investigation was instigated and it was quickly established that the complaints all centred around the northern Cheviot Hills, in the Northumberland National Park.

A close study of the high resolution maps available indicated that the area under scrutiny was open countryside. There weren't any buildings or facilities able to generate a signal that could cause the disruption that was being experienced. There must be something there, even though the maps state that there wasn't.

The definitive answer could only be obtained by sending a drone over the area to collect some images. The almost silent drone completed its mission and returned to base, allowing its precious cargo of images to be collected. These were transferred to the main computer in London, without any incident and early next morning the images were examined.

The majority of the images matched the map, displaying open countryside, whereas one area was of more interest. The drone struggled to remain on course, although the compensation circuitry managed to keep it close to the pre-programmed course, allowing it to only deviate by a small amount. From the images obtained, it was obvious that a large, black, corrugated warehouse existed, although it didn't appear on any map.

The most convincing evidence was that as the warehouse was approached the images became corrupted. The image that was recorded when the drone flew over it was completely obliterated and as the drone passed by, the quality of the image returned to normal quality.

Despite exhaustive enquiries the owner of the warehouse wasn't identified. There was only one course of action available to them and that was to examine the structure for themselves. Such an operation required sanctioning and after the reason, along with the evidence provided by the images were presented, approval was given. A team was assembled, covering the various disciplines thought to be required for the operation.

Two days later, following a high speed, low level flight, the team assembled at the warehouse doors. In the meantime, the military contingent had scanned the area around the warehouse, looking for booby traps, buried ordnance and any other access points. On their return they gave the all-clear. The locksmith was now called into action. His task was to open the large brass padlock that secured the doors. He noted that the padlock didn't appear to have been used recently and managed to release it in a couple of minutes. He placed the padlock into his toolkit and stepped back, making way for the person who would open the doors. The hinges squeaked as the doors were opened, presenting them with a sight that they weren't prepared for.

They were confronted by a large steel door, that was set into an extremely solid wall. Upon investigation, it was quickly established that the corrugated warehouse construction was, in fact, a shell that fitted over a new building and masked its presence.

In the centre of the door was a push-button locking system. The locksmith stated that it wasn't the most up-to-date, although breaking the code could take a great deal of time. He took a close look at the lock and tentatively pushed a couple of buttons, then turned to the team leader and said, "I think this will take longer than the padlock!" He then rummaged through his kit to establish whether he had the correct electronic equipment to enable him to break the lock code.

When the locksmith depressed the key pad buttons, a red light began to flash on a monitoring board many miles away. A video signal was automatically displayed on a large monitor, so that the cause of the alarm could be seen. The operative contacted his superior, to explain the reason for an alarm signal.

"Is it kids again?"

"Not this time, Sir, it looks like a task force and by the look of them, I think that they're determined to get inside."

"Re-set the alarm and keep an eye on them. Contact me again

in a couple of hours and update me on any developments."

"Yes, Sir, will do."

The PA system burst into life: "Team 6, get ready for deployment! Possible breach at Repository 11." It only took a few minutes for the six men chosen for the operation to gather together. The sergeant assigned to lead the operation had a few things to say before they set off.

"I'm pleased to see that you're displaying your radiation badges. Have you replacements, in case the others become tainted? Good! You know what Repository 11 is like and you've seen the results of carelessness. Take care! I don't want any of you ending up like that. This is an observation mission, so there's no need to get too close to the building. Those that are there will soon begin to feel the effects of the radiation and will hopefully call for help. All that we're asked to do is watch what is taking place and there shouldn't be any need for us to intervene. Any questions? Good, let's get going."

They had to land some distance from their intended target, as they didn't want to announce their arrival. This meant that they had a good distance of cross-country walking ahead of them, especially as they needed to keep from the skyline and the possibility of being observed. As they approached the final hilltop they dropped down onto their hands and knees and finally crawled on their stomachs. Keeping very flat, they peered over the hilltop and observed their target. But there were only three men there.

After arriving at the corrugated warehouse and performing the ensuing reconnaissance, it was decided to leave three men on site: two soldiers and the locksmith, while the remainder of the team withdrew and established a temporary base, within walking distance. In the meantime, a second locksmith was summoned from the main base to allow an interchange of personnel.

The locksmith was busy trying to break the code and the two soldiers were wandering about aimlessly.

"Look over here, I've found a four-leaf clover."

"Only one? I've found a clump of them over here."

This discovery encouraged them to study the grass around the area a little closer. They found a wide selection of deviations from the normal: blades of grass that split like a snake's tongue, a single daisy that had two stalks and so the variations continued.

"There's something weird about this place, it puts me on edge," one soldier said. At this point, the locksmith headed towards them. They thought that he was just stretching his legs, but not this time.

"I'm not feeling very well," he said.

Both soldiers noticed his radiation patch at the same time, it had turned ominously black.

"I think we should get out of here," the senior soldier said. "Your radiation patch has turned black."

"Have you looked at your own patches recently?" the locksmith asked. Immediately both soldiers looked down at their patches; theirs had also turned black. "I think that we should make a rapid exit from this place," and he pressed the panic button on his communicator.

The three of them headed for the temporary base camp and soon realised that they were feeling very tired and weak. By the time that they met the medical team, the locksmith was having to be supported by the two soldiers. It was explained to them that the locksmith was in the worst condition, as he had been closer to the source of the radiation. They were placed on anti-grav stretchers and by the time that they returned to the base camp, a personnel transporter, staffed by a medical team, was waiting for the three of them. They were placed inside and the transport took off, heading for the military hospital at their home base.

A small team was assembled to return to the warehouse, to fasten the outside doors and refit the original padlock, which was undamaged by the locksmith. They were assured that they wouldn't be affected by the radiation as the time spent in proximity to the source would be extremely limited.

The officer in charge of the task force, Major Stephen Harcourt, was fuming. Three of his men had been injured trying to gain access to a seemingly ordinary warehouse. "I will be asking questions about this place," he said to his second in command. "No wonder members of the public have been having problems. I want to know what is stored in that building and who is behind its creation. That building is dangerous!"

The order was given to break camp and transports were requested to return the personnel, along with all their kit, back to the base station. During the journey, Major Harcourt continued to breathe fire and brimstone, aimed at those responsible for the whole debacle. "Someone is responsible for this and I intend to identify them and demand a full explanation!"

The surveillance team had to remain in place, until they received a message informing them that the task force was out of the area. They didn't want a simple mistake to reveal their presence at this late stage. They met back at the assembly point and awaited their transport back to base. Once there, they were able to make their reports and conclusions. It was assumed that the officer in charge of the task force wouldn't be happy with the outcome of his attempts to get inside the warehouse and there would be efforts made, on his part, to ascertain the purpose of the building and to establish what was stored there.

As Major Harcourt entered the base, on the following morning, he had two items circulating in his mind. Rather than heading to his office, he used one of the electric trolleys to drive to the opposite side of the base, where the infirmary was located.

After identifying himself, he was directed to the ward where his men from the aborted mission, a couple of days earlier, were being cared for. They were pleased to see him, even though he had to wear anti-radiation clothing. The two soldiers were not feeling too bad, but the locksmith was in a bad way. Major Harcourt decided that the only way to get an accurate assessment of their condition was to speak to the doctor overseeing their treatment.

"Come in," the doctor called out, as the Major knocked on the door. Following the introductions, the doctor asked the first question. "Where on earth did you take those men?"

"Actually, it was Northumberland. I know they don't have the best weather in that part of the country, but I didn't think it was detrimental to anyone's wellbeing!"

"Well, Major, the radiation that's affected your men is most unusual. Our treatment for radiation has improved greatly over the years and the investigation relies on the identification of the source of the contamination. We now have a large database of radiation types, but in your men's case, that's all proved useless."

"What exactly does that mean for the three sick men in the ward?" Major Harcourt asked.

"What I'm saying in a roundabout way," the doctor replied, "is that the radiation that has made your men sick, does not originate on any planet that man has visited. So I don't have any idea where it originates from."

"Very funny," Major Harcourt replied. "Have you been told to withhold the truth from me?"

"Certainly not! I don't have any idea where the radiation has come from, that has made your men ill. Are you sure that you've only been to Northumberland?" asked the doctor.

"It appears that someone has withheld the truth from both of us, if we are telling the truth, as I believe we both are. I don't have any reason to withhold information from you, doctor and I don't believe you have anything to gain by withholding information from me. All I want is to have my men in good health and ready for duty again."

"I think we should work together to discover who's withholding information, because until we find out the truth, you're not going to get your men back in good health and I'll be faced with the problem again. Let's agree to work together and sort this out. Agreed Major?"

"Agreed doctor."

They shook hands, forming a pact between them.

CHAPTER 6

WORDS SPOKEN IN A BAR

By the time Santos and Javan arrived at the space port bar the entertainment had already commenced. As they walked in Santos scanned the room for a suitable table, while Javan went to the bar to collect the first drinks of the evening.

The entertainment was being provided by a group of musicians gathered from a variety of farms, scattered across Nivarna 7. As each couple walked in, they started to sway to the music even before their coats had been removed.

Before long, the place was heaving with people, most of them dancing, but some groups gathering around tables.

"Are you coming to have a dance?" Javan asked of his companion.

"No way," Santos replied. "I'm too old for that carry on. What about a fine young man like you? There's plenty of ladies to ask for a dance, why not give it a go?"

"No thanks. I'll sit here and watch everyone dancing and enjoy the music. After all, that band is rather good!"

"Well, I suppose they're better than the recorded stuff we normally get."

"You're a stuffy old thing, Santos! Anyway, I may be young, but I've seen too many fights start at dances and I don't intend to wake tomorrow morning with a black eye, so I'll sit and watch."

The evening was progressing nicely, when the master of ceremonies got up onto the stage and asked the band to stop playing. It took some of the dancers a few moments to realise that the music had stopped and to turn towards the stage and ascertain what was taking place.

"Ladies and Gentlemen, I'm sorry to interrupt your evening," the MC said, "but I have just been informed of a sad incidence. Sybert, of Central Farm 3, whom I'm sure you all know, has been found dead in what can only be described as suspicious circumstances. The Nivarna police will be with us very shortly and have asked that you all remain here in the interim. Thank you for paying attention, so please enjoy the rest of the evening as best as you can, under the circumstances." He then asked the band to continue and they actually played the best set they ever had, although the audience didn't seem to be in the mood any more so the band gave up playing after about forty minutes.

Following the MC's announcement, there wasn't any enthusiasm for dancing or even chatting. Everyone began to gather in groups to discuss what had taken place and who could possibly be to blame. They were worried. Could they be the next victim? The perpetrator needed to be found and quickly. If they were honest, they already had someone in mind and a number of other people had also arrived at the same conclusion.

"Don't look now, but people are staring at us from all around the room!"

"I know," replied Javan, "I was expecting this to happen. I've already experienced a similar situation a couple of times in the past. As I'm a stranger, I'm the first to be blamed, but you'll find that as soon as the problem is dealt with, everything will revert to normal."

Javan continued. "Don't stare back at them, as that tends to antagonise and will rile and anger them. Let's keep out of it." The two friends continued their conversation, supped their drinks and tried to ascertain who was to blame for the heinous crime.

Fortunately, a Nivarna police team were in the vicinity and arrived within two hours. As they walked into the bar, the place became silent. Everyone turned to look at them. They wore the standard NP uniform, which consisted of black heavy-duty shoes, navy trousers and a collarless sand-coloured jacket, emblazoned with a name tag and various other badges.

The team was led by Inspector Helena Banwick; tall, slim and in her late thirties, with striking ash-blonde hair, cut in the latest style. She quickly took charge of the situation and, along with her five officers, started to list the names and details of all those present. Most of those given the opportunity to voice their suspicions of Javan did so when approached by an officer.

Santos and Javan were left until last and were dealt with by the inspector. She suggested that for his own safety, it might be advisable for Javan to be temporarily incarcerated until the whole situation calmed down. She impressed on him, that this was only a temporary measure and that he wasn't under suspicion and would be released as soon as it was practical.

The two of them stood up and walked towards the exit, while a slow handclap gradually increased in volume. As they walked through the door, Santos stopped, turned and shouted. "Shame on you. Shame on you all!"

As they entered the corridor, the inspector turned to Javan, saying, "I'm sorry about all the unpleasantness."

"Don't worry, it's happened to me in the past and will most likely happen again," said Javan, with a slight smile at the corners of his mouth.

Javan was locked in the cell and Santos spoke to him through the intercom. "I'll be back to see you tomorrow son. I know for sure that you didn't have anything to do with the death of Sybert and will fight for you every step of the way."

Once all the documentation was completed, Javan was left on his own. As he laid back on his bed he said to himself: 'Here we go again.'

The following day everything began to change. Some unexpected information began to appear on the Nivarna news net. This was to turn the whole situation upside down and to instigate the freeing of Javan from the NP cell. The whole Nivarna planetary system was in turmoil. The night that Sybert was found dead on Nivarna 7, a similar occurrence had taken place on each of the other eleven planets.

The revelation completely changed the tenor of the NP investigations. They now had twelve murders to be solved and decided to investigate the background of each of the victims and complete a thorough post mortem.

The medical examinations highlighted a very unusual cause of death; the victims all looked as if they had been struck on the head by a hard object, but that wasn't the case. Rather than finding an indentation in the skull, a piece of the skull had actually been blown out, due to a build up of pressure from inside the skull, without any external marks on the head.

Investigations inside confirmed this conclusion. It was as if the brain had been boiled inside the skull, the pressure building, until the brain burst out anyway that it could.

The pathologist, Professor McMillan, was so astounded by his findings that he asked fellow doctors if they could confirm his conclusions. As more doctors became involved information began to leak out, instigating a visit from unannounced government officials. The pathologist soon realised that the investigation he had just undertaken was more important than he had realised.

He was tidying up at the end of the day, when the government team arrived. He was shown, briefly, an identification badge and official-looking papers, granting the team authorisation to remove anything involved with the twelve victims. The team split up into two distinct units, one going through the paperwork, including the information on any computer unit. While the other team, placed each of the bodies into black bags, zipped them up and sealed them shut.

I'll give them one thing, the pathologist thought as he sat quietly in his office, they're highly efficient! Thirty minutes later, all traces of the bodies had been removed and the tables had been hosed and scrubbed down.

The information gatherers took longer. After all, they had a great deal more to search through. Eventually their trawl was completed and the majority of the team left the building, carrying sheets of paper and boxes full of information discs. The few remaining members continued with the far more complex computer searches, eventually being satisfied that every trace of the post mortems had been eradicated from the systems. As they collected their equipment together the official apparently in charge, approached the pathologist and informed him that their business was completed.

"Are you leaving paperwork that covers the removal of the bodies and all the information that you've collected?" the pathologist asked. "I had to sign for everything. How am I to explain the disappearance of twelve bodies? Especially as they arrived here under very unusual circumstances!" He was handed a card, bearing the name and contact details of a government department that he'd never heard of.

"If anyone asks any questions, tell them to contact this department," the official said. Then they all departed and silence descended upon the path lab.

The pathologist stood up, removed his white coat, placed it on a coat hook and put on his jacket. Leaving his office, he extinguished the light and noticed a couple of scrunched up pieces of paper on the floor by the end of a desk. He took the opportunity to bend down to pick them up and surreptitiously checked the bottom of his trouser leg. He felt a reassuring bump in the lining. This was done very carefully, as he felt that he was under surveillance, from cameras left by the government team. They didn't trust him and he didn't trust them either.

The following morning, Professor McMillan, visited his bank and was cordially greeted. "I'd like access to my safety deposit box, please," he requested.

"Take a seat and I'll arrange for someone to help you," the young woman said.

A few minutes later he was guided down the stairs to the vault and then into the area that housed the private security boxes. The use of keys had been abandoned years ago and had been replaced by thumb print readers. The cubicle door clicked shut behind him as the bank official left. The Professor now had security and lifted his left foot onto the chair. Expanding a slight tear in the seam at the extremity of his trouser leg, an information stick was extracted and placed into the security box.

When he'd first been approached to take on the unusual task, he realised that it was an extraordinary case and had recorded all of the autopsies, along with any other relevant information. That little information stick cost very little, but the data that it contained was worth a fortune and could cost his life.

CHAPTER 7

TRANSPORT 113

The last two containers from Nivarna 10 were loaded onto Transport 113, completing the payload from N10. The transport was now full to capacity. The next port of call would be Earth base, so the crew started to prepare for the long journey ahead.

When all of the formalities were completed the pilot contacted Nivarna control, seeking permission to move away from the loading station. Permission was granted and the message concluded by wishing the crew a safe journey back to Earth. The manoeuvring thrusters burst into life and the huge craft began to slowly pull away.

The four-person crew used this time in preparation for the impending journey. The pilot and co-pilot checked the ship systems and ran some diagnostic programmes through the computer, the navigator ensured that the computer at his station was correctly programmed for the journey back to Earth and the payload engineer ensured that all of the containers were secure and ready for the journey. Then as the thrusters dropped out, the mass of the ship kept it moving in the direction it had attained.

Finally, it was far enough away from the planet to enable the main engines to be ignited and Transport 113 slowly began to increase its speed. The crew ensured that everything was working as it should and then the control systems were switched to automatic.

Each crew had its own habits and practices; this particular crew liked to settle down to a hearty meal, once the main engines had been ignited and the ship's systems switched to auto. This tended to relax them all and if there were any new crew members, it helped them all to get to know one another. At times the dining room became quite raucous, but it helped to set them all at ease.

By the time the meal was almost completed, the ship had speedily travelled a huge distance, leaving Nivarna 10 far behind. The navigation computer was now directing the ship and the powerful engines were still slowly increasing the ship's speed. It's almost impossible to comprehend the velocity they were travelling at, but it was required as the distance that they were to cover was vast.

The noise level in the dining room had subsided dramatically as the crew relaxed after enjoying their meal. Eventually they would leave, move to their individual bedrooms and sleep off the effects of the large meal that they'd just enjoyed. They were shaken out of the dozy state that they'd sunk into by the sounding of an alarm signal. Instantly they all were wide awake and alert.

"That's the proximity alarm!" the pilot said.

"What could possibly be out here?" the navigator asked. "We've travelled this route dozens of times and never had any problems before."

They rushed along the corridor that led to the control room and had to allow their eyes to adjust to the low level red light that was used in there. The pilot slipped into his seat on the control deck and re-set the proximity alarm, which also silenced it, much to everyone's relief. He also lifted a clear cover from over a red triangular button.

"Remind me what that button is for?" the navigator asked. "I should know, but I've forgotten for the moment."

"That's the interstellar alarm," the pilot replied. "It attempts to connect us with any nearby Nivarna planet, or any of the communication satellites that are spread throughout the sector. Although we may not be able to establish voice communication, it will transmit a 'Transport in Trouble' signal which carries our identification code."

By now, everyone's eyes had adjusted to the light level and were able to clearly see outside. They were astounded by what they saw. Running parallel with the transport was a huge craft, at least four times the size of the transport. They were all stunned into silence. They'd never seen anything like it before, neither had any other human. The pilot cast an eye over the control panel just to see if the alarm button had ceased to flash and had become a steady light, which would mean that the system had been able to make a connection. Unfortunately, that hadn't happened.

The silence was broken by the payload engineer. "Look at the size of that thing. I hope they're friendly, 'cause we haven't any way to defend ourselves. I hate to think what kind of weapons they have."

The words were barely out of his lips when two huge searchlights came alive on the alien craft. They began to sweep over the transport, one from each end. Silence settled over the control room once again, as each of the crew members tried to ascertain what would happen next. They were all so engrossed with what was taking place outside, that they failed to notice that the emergency transmitter was emitting a steady light, meaning that it had contacted a receiver, tuned to the appropriate frequency.

As the beams of the two searchlights became closer together, a high-pitched noise increased inside the transport, until just before convergence it became almost unbearable. The two beams coincided and the noise in the ship caused the crew to lose consciousness, just before the transport exploded into a cloud of debris. The alien ship extinguished the two beams and moved away in an unbelievable burst of speed.

The distress call transmitted by Transport 113, was picked up by a nearby communication satellite, boosted and retransmitted to the closest planet, which happened to be Nivarna 4.

The instant the system indicated a distress call, the operator on Nivarna 4 was able to identify the origin of the source of the signal, but when the signal was lost after a few seconds, she realised that something dire had taken place. She immediately contacted the Nivarna police, as they had ships that were speedy and able to rescue any survivors.

The route of the transport ships was well documented and with the time that the distress call was received, it enabled the position of the transport when the disaster occurred to be quickly established. A crew was assembled and a ship was soon launched, to hunt for Transport 113. They didn't head directly for the transport route, as they had to allow for the drift caused by the speed the transport was travelling at when the problem occurred.

Eventually, they arrived at the point which was the source of the distress call and the long-range radar was switched on receiving a weak signal from a point in the distance. As they honed in on the point, the image on the screen slowly grew, although it was far too large to be a transport. They finally arrived at a large cloud of debris, which they identified as Transport 113. It was obvious that something catastrophic had overtaken the craft, destroying it totally, removing any chance of survivors.

The Nivarna Police craft circled the debris cloud and recorded a sequence of images to include in the report to Nivarna Control, back on Earth. It was pointless to even consider a salvage operation, as the transport and its payload was totally destroyed, having been reduced to tiny segments.

When the report was received on Earth, the only comment that was made to the committee was, "I'm not surprised. I was expecting this, especially under the current circumstances." The report was stamped 'Top Secret' and placed into a safe, along with a number of similarly designated documents.

The Nivarna planets were like a big family and news such as the destruction of a transport, quickly spread through the communities like fire through dry grass. A great deal of angry discussion took place and many different courses of action were discussed, although a definitive solution wasn't ever reached.

CHAPTER 8

STIRRING THE POT

"... So that's the situation that we are facing. I do realise that this must have been a shock to many of you, but everything presented to you this evening has been obtained from official government documents. How things will develop in the future is unsure, although each and everyone of us will be affected in some way. Thank you for your time this evening, and good fortune to you all."

Within moments of the broadcast's conclusion, each member of the Nivarna operative committee was contacted via their communication devices. The message they received was a summons to gather at the Off-world department building, where the committee had a secure office, a rare place where they held their meetings without fear of being overheard, or having their electronic communications intercepted.

The security department was also working flat out, checking the names that had any involvement in the programme, from the narrator to the colourist. It was noticed that those who appeared "on camera" had their images distorted in such a fashion that it wasn't visually apparent, but prevented facial recognition systems being able to lock in on them. When this was realised, the team began to concentrate on the locations used and the flora and fauna that were apparent in the images.

By trying to ascertain the smallest details in the scenes of the programme, could help them in two ways. First of all, to pin down where the film was made and secondly assisting them in identifying the team that had assembled the transmitted material. The fact that every statement made in the broadcast was absolutely true wasn't the concern of the security department, they wanted to find out who had produced the broadcast and nothing more. Denying the truth was a subject that the committee was going to have to deal with.

It was one in the morning when the committee assembled, only one person was missing. The chairman was late, as usual.

René Smythe was a large man in his mid-sixties, who was confined to an anti-gravity invalid chair, as he'd been involved in an accident some years before. An accident was one version that did the rounds, along with various other accounts. Smythe never discussed what it was that caused him to end up disabled and those that had taken a chance and asked him, still bore the scars from the encounter.

The chairman called them to order and thanked them all for attending at such short notice, even though their attendance was demanded and the meeting was officially opened. To start things off, the head of the security department was invited to report on his department's findings, so far.

"On the few occasions that a face appears on screen, the image has been subtly distorted, somehow, so that facial recognition systems are unable to make an identification. That being the case, we turned our attention to the list of names on the credits. This also turned out to be a dead end. None of the names appear anywhere on the world-wide population listings. As far as we are able to ascertain they are all false names. At present, the only course left open to us is to examine the broadcast frame by frame, to see if we are able to uncover any hidden codes or subliminal messages. Apart from this final course of action, there isn't much more we can do. But we will keep searching for the key to unlock this puzzle, such as who commissioned the broadcast in the first place."

The chairman thanked him for his report. "I was hoping that you clever bods would have been able to dig up something that would have set us on the path to solving the problem we face. I'm sure that your team has contacts that you can call on to delve into some of the dark corners that exist in our society. Who knows what you'll find lurking in those places that the majority of the population avoid."

A general conversation ensued, with the first delegate to speak suggesting the tracking down those who had access to the information that was used in the broadcast. He felt that it would be a group of people, rather than an individual and, once identified, the security department would be able to check them out. Also looking for any affiliations to any subversive groups and if any such links exited, they could form the key that would open up the way to establish who it was that had made the broadcast.

He paused, looking around the room to see how his comments had been received. He was just about to start speaking again, when the bomb exploded. So powerful was the explosion that it didn't only kill all those in the room, but it also blew out the walls and destroyed the adjacent rooms above and below as well. It may have been early in the morning, but all hell broke loose. People were running everywhere, sprinkler systems were triggered and alarm bells started ringing. Members of the public who were walking past the building, had to dodge the pieces of falling masonry and office furniture. Within moments fire engines arrived and elite police security officers appeared on the scene. Such an incident, the bombing of a government building, would not go unnoticed and the news broadcast crews were quickly on scene, gathering footage for the morning's news programmes and lead stories.

Within twenty minutes or so of the blast occurring, the 24-hours news broadcasters had reporters on the scene gathering every scrap of information available. These were soon joined by the reporters from the overseas' companies sending news all over the world. As the breakfast programmes were prepared these reports were spliced in along with the latest news that had been gathered, with interviewees that were available.

The story was also carried by Nivarna Net, who provided the evening telecast to all of the Nivarna planets. It wasn't received with a great deal of sympathy, the general feeling being that it was about time that Earth had to deal with the kind of problem that the various Nivarna planets had been suffering for a long time now. Anyway, they were still smarting following the destruction of Transport 113 and the lack of investigation by the Earth's authorities.

The problem was that all of the unusual occurrences that had been taking place on the various Nivarna planets, were never reported to the people on Earth. This was a specific decision of the Nivarna operating committee, who had just been extinguished and the inhabitants of the Nivarna planets weren't sorry to see them go. It was their actions that had prevented any support growing for them as each incident occurred. As long as the deliveries of food kept arriving was all they were concerned with.

This was the kind of situation, when anti-Earth feeling was at its peak, that the more militant among the farmers had been waiting for. Their leader had wild red hair and was a farmer on Nivarna 1. He originated from Scottish stock and went by the name of Hamish Hamilton, a mountain of a man who had a definite course of action in mind. He'd already convinced the majority of farmers on his own planet and felt ready to spread his message among the rest of the planets.

With a fiery brand of rhetoric, that would rouse the most peaceable of men, he sent his message out over the interplanetary network, then sat back and awaited the response which, when received, was exactly as he'd expected and wanted. From right across the system he received comments that were supportive of his point of view.

He then suggested that, subject to approval by each planet's council, a gathering of delegates from all twelve planets should decide the course of action to take, that would demonstrate to earth that they were not willing to put up with all of the adverse incidents that had been taking place and be left to deal with the outcome themselves. After all, they were farmers not security officers. The decision of the delegates would be sent to Earth and the Nivarna system would await their response.

CHAPTER 9

CONFLICTING OPINIONS

The majority of the planets were pleased to receive the message from Nivarna 1. They had harboured similar feelings for a long time, but didn't have the nerve to set the ball rolling. Now that someone else was willing to take the lead, they were quite ready to fall in line.

Not everyone was as quick to jump on the bandwagon. Three planets: Nos. 3, 8 and 11 were concerned about being encouraged to take part in a course of action that they weren't happy with. They'd all heard charismatic speakers before, who seemed able to talk their audience into any course of action that they were promoting. So they decided to meet together to iron out their position, before the system-wide meeting took place and select delegates that would speak on behalf of them.

Of course, their actions did not go unnoticed. Nirvana 1 had its informants throughout the system, feeding the actions and feelings of all the other planets back to Hamish. He didn't want any surprises on the day that all the delegates assembled. He needed to be kept up to date with all the developments, so that he could adjust his approach to have the maximum effect on his audience.

The three cautious planets arranged their meeting for two weeks before the system-wide gathering. They decided to meet on Nivarna 8, as it had the best facilities to cope with all the delegates. Each planet made its arrangements, deciding who was going to speak on their behalf and put their point of view over in the most beneficial way. Trying to avoid drawing attention to themselves, No. 3 and 11 made their own individual arrangements for travel to the three-planet gathering.

By the time everything was arranged, travel, speeches and an accompanying list of delegates, it was only a couple of days before the meeting. The work of the delegates on their home planets was to be covered by other farmers and their helpers until they returned home. The growing and care of the crops had to continue, even if they weren't on site at the time. This was a characteristic of the support each planet's farmers were willing to give to one another.

As the delegates arrived, they were ushered into the meeting space that had been prepared for them, the volume slowly increasing as each group of delegates arrived. Finally, everyone was assembled, the doors were closed and guards were placed on sentry duty outside. It was expected that spies would be placed in the meeting. It didn't take long to uncover the intruders and they were unceremoniously removed from the meeting, to a chorus made up of various catcalls and insults.

Each of the Nivarna planets had some incarceration cells, which were usually used to restrain fighting famers, those who had imbibed a little too much ale, along with anyone else who became a little too boisterous. The two spies were subjected to a very thorough strip search, along with an electronic scan designed to locate any implanted devices. Once the searches were completed they were locked up in individual cells, only to be released once the meeting had been concluded and the visiting delegates were on their way back to their own planets. The Nivarna police were then to be called in and told that they could do what they wanted with the two miscreants.

An attractive dark-haired woman stepped up on the small platform at the end of the room to be greeted by whistles and other displays of appreciation.

"Hello everybody," she said. "Thank you for such a wonderful greeting. I'm Dagmar Perovic and I'm to be the chairwoman of this meeting. The pairs of delegates were asked to come up onto the platform, where six chairs had been set out. As they rose from their seats and made their way to the platform, they were heartily applauded and cheered. Once they were settled on their chairs, Dagmar stepped forward to officially get the meeting underway.

"I know that you're a bunch of simple farmers so..." her voice was drowned out by whistles and jeers. "Well, it's good that you haven't lost your sense of humour," she said to them, this comment being met with widespread applause. As this subsided,

Dagmar continued to speak. “Let’s try to keep a light-hearted feel to the proceedings and not get too irate with one another.”

At this point a member of the audience stood up. “I’d like to make a comment,” he said.

“Please go ahead,” Dagmar replied.

The man was handed a microphone and began to speak. “By all means keep things light-hearted, but don’t forget that we’re here to discuss a very serious matter, the outcome of which could affect the future of the Nivarna planets. So we don’t need to become so upright that we come to blows, just because we have differing opinions. Be tolerant and treat one another with respect. Thank you.” He then sat down and handed the microphone to the attendant. The room was silent, then applause began to ring out until the volume of it was almost overwhelming.

By the time a consensus was reached, they were well into the afternoon of the second allocated day. Miss Perovic rose from her chair to make an announcement.

“Ladies and gentlemen, we’ll take a break for a few moments now, while the delegates and I write up the decisions that we have reached. When we assemble again, I’ll read the document out to you. If everyone here is happy with the wording, each delegate on the platform will be given a copy, to take back to your respective planets. We decided that would be the best way to ensure that everyone would be able to read the document, without having too many copies in circulation. See you back here after the break.”

About twenty-five minutes later they all drifted back into the room and returned to their seats. When they were all settled, the doors were closed and the guards took their positions. Dagmar walked onto the stage and was greeted once again with expressions of appreciation from the audience.

“Thank you for that wonderful greeting,” she said. “If you’ll all settle down now, I’ll read the document that sums up the decisions we’ve made over the last couple of days.”

She then read out the contents of the document that could well restrain Hamish’s more outlandish plans. Basically, it said that the residents of Nivarna 3, 8 and 11, all agreed that Earth had to take notice of the problems that the Nivarna planets had been putting up with, without any assistance whatsoever from Earth's forces and they'd basically had enough. The only course of action they wouldn't go along with was anything that involved violence.

The conclusion of Dagmar's reading was met with applause from the audience, then she said, "I would just like you to please applaud again if you are happy with the document and its contents."

The building erupted with that noise of the applause, coupled with whistles, shouts and stamping feet. The volume was so incredible, that it was amazing that the windows weren't blown out, but they managed to withstand the assault.

"Thank you, everyone," Dagmar struggled to say over the noise, which slowly subsided. "Copies will be distributed to my six friends who have shared the platform with me. So that sadly brings this exceptional meeting to its conclusion. Thank you all so much for making the effort to get here; I know that it can't have been easy. Just one final thought to take home with you – what we've discussed over the last couple of days is private to our three planets and there are those out there who would love to find out what we've been talking about. It's up to each one of us to ensure that they don't find out. Thank you and goodbye to you all."

That was it, their special meeting was over and they began to make their way home, never realising what a surprise the system meeting would be.

CHAPTER 10

SPECULATION AND SUSPICION

Following the aborted attempt by the task force to establish the contents of the warehouse in Northumberland, Major Harcourt, and Dr McAndrew, the doctor charged with caring for the soldiers with radiation sickness, had been asking some very awkward questions. Each one of them had been summoned to their superior's office and had been asked in a very subtle way to cease their investigations. When they refused and backed up their refusals with solid reasoning, the attitude of their respective interviewer changed completely: from a friendly request to a veiled warning, to keep away from matters that didn't concern them. Despite their individual protestations, they were told to expect repercussions if they didn't. It was as if the two superiors involved were working from the same script, which only added to the conviction that the questions that Major Harcourt and the doctor were asking were pressing the right buttons and causing concern among those involved.

* * *

The sleek anti-grav car turned off of the country road onto a concrete driveway. About a hundred yards along there was a security man's hut accompanied by a liftable barrier across the road. As he saw the car turn onto the drive, the security officer stepped out, ready to check the paperwork of the car's passenger. The driver presented the paperwork to the security officer, who checked the details against the list on his clipboard, then handed the papers back to the driver and gave him instructions concerning where his passenger was to be taken. The barrier across the road was raised and the car drove slowly through. The security officer saluted as the car passed by, then closed the barrier. The passenger was somewhat bemused by this, as he'd never been saluted before.

As the car approached a group of buildings it became apparent that the facility was an abandoned airfield and from the condition of the various buildings it was obvious that it hadn't been used for some time.

Why was I ordered to report here? The passenger thought to himself, although the location and name of 'here' was never mentioned. Am I to be abandoned in the middle of this old airfield? But if that's the case, why send such a posh car for me? Question after question ran through his mind and most frustratingly, he didn't have an answer for any of them.

The car pulled up outside a hut that had obviously been refurbished, maybe especially for this event. There were other similar cars parked outside the building, each one unloading their passenger, or in some cases passengers. The driver of each vehicle carried the single bag that each passenger had been instructed to bring, loaded with the necessities, set out on a list included with their orders. He followed his driver through the swing doors into the vestibule just inside the doors. There were a couple of soldiers standing behind a small counter, their function was to collect the holdalls from the driver, who also handed over an envelope which was placed under the counter, along with all the others collected so far.

Once the procedure had been completed, his driver directed him through the swing doors that led into the main area of the building. He thanked the driver for his assistance and walked over to the doors. The age of the doors was obvious from the old style windows fitted in them. They were circular, not unlike a porthole on a ship.

As he stood looking through one of the windows, one of the soldiers asked, "Is everything all right, Sir?"

"Umm, yes, thank you. I was just trying to see if I recognised anyone before I entered the room."

"That's okay, Sir, take all the time you need, there's only one more person to come now, then you'll need to go inside for the welcoming speech," the soldier replied.

As he turned back to the viewing window, the crowd temporarily parted and at the back of the room he saw a face that he recognised. He pushed the door open and stepped in. The gathering wasn't as extensive as he had thought, neither was the room in which they were meeting. He worked his way around those assembled, taking care as he went as most of them had drinks in their hands and headed towards the one person that he knew.

The group of three didn't pay much attention when he sidled over to them, continuing their conversation which basically consisted of speculation about the reason for gathering them together. While he stood there a steward approached him and asked if he would like drink.

"A strong black coffee," he replied.

The member of the trio that had his back to him turned. "I thought I recognised that voice. What are you doing here, Doc?"

"I could ask you the same question, Stephen."

The two friends briefly embraced and then the introductions began. Each one of the quartet relayed a similar story: sealed orders had been dispatched to them, informing of a change of assignment, but without details of either where or what it was. The only detail was the time and date for a car to arrive which would transport them. The fact that a car was being sent for them, was what caused most speculation and, under the circumstances, they weren't able to discuss it with anyone, not even their superior officers.

"May I have your attention, please," a voice said, from the opposite end of the room. The undertone of conversation died down and everyone turned to look towards the source of the voice. There was a low-level stage about two feet high and on it stood a grey-haired man, dressed in a classy suit and tie.

"Would you all please take a seat and I will explain the basics about this gathering. Then there will be a break for lunch, which has been prepared in the room next door. Later on a military officer will explain the more confidential aspects of this project. I'm afraid I'm unable to tell you any more, as I'm not conversant with the details myself. The group that has been gathered here today is basically made up of three elements: scientific, military and medical. We'll start with the medical. There's one doctor, who is assisted by four nurses, who have been trained to paramedic level. Together they form a highly competent team."

Stephen Harcourt, who was sitting next to the doctor, jabbed his friend with his elbow and said, "Never thought of you as being highly competent before," and he chuckled.

"At least I have some nurses to work with," the Doctor replied.

"You jammy sod," was all that Stephen said in reply.

The military unit was next to be mentioned, led by Major Harcourt along with a variety of other ranks. Details of the scientific team were to be dealt with during the afternoon session, along with the nature of the project they had all been assigned to, which was a subject that they all were very interested in. Especially as up to now, the subject had not been touched on at all. There was an audible sigh of relief, when it was announced that there would now be a break for lunch, especially as some of the assembled group had been travelling since early in the morning.

It wasn't surprising that the two friends sat together, while they enjoyed the meal that was provided for them. As they were eating the pudding, Doug turned to his companion and said, "Don't you think it's a little strange that you and I were chosen for this assignment? After all, there were plenty of 'golden boys' who could have been chosen, who haven't been hauled over the coals for asking awkward questions?"

"I'm so glad that you mentioned it," Stephen replied. "I thought that I was being paranoid, thinking that way. It's a relief to realise that you are thinking along the same lines as I am."

"Good," Doug replied, "there must be some reason why we've been allocated onto such a prestigious operation. I can't help but feel there's some ulterior motive behind our being here!"

"Excuse me, gents." They both looked up, in response to the voice from the other side of the table. "I'm sorry, but I couldn't help overhearing your conversation, especially as I seem to be in the same boat as you two are. Oh, by the way, my name is Chris Dent and I'm a lab technician, working on one of the many sub-projects involved in all of this. It seems that all of the groups have been working on sections of the project, although no one seems to know what it is. That's where I fell foul of the authorities, by asking too many probing questions. They, whoever they are, didn't appreciate my inquisitiveness and so I was given verbal lashing for my cheek."

"This is beginning to have a familiar pattern to it," said Stephen. "I wonder how many others, gathered here, are like us?"

"Maybe they're too frightened to say anything," Doug replied. "Anyway, they're all drifting back into the main hall now. Maybe we'll learn something more this afternoon, so we need to keep our eyes and ears open and see if we can make any further contact. By the way, I'm Doug," said the doctor.

"I'm Stephen. Nice to meet you, Chris. Welcome to our exclusive little club."

CHAPTER 11

DECISION TIME

"Are you sure that you'll be able to manage on your own?"

"No problem. After all, I've been working alongside you for months now and, anyway, the equipment used nowadays is all computer and GPS controlled. It's not like farming from Earth's history, when they had to use horses and everything had to be performed manually. So there's nothing to worry about."

"I'll take your word for it. Anyhow I won't be here to keep my eye on you, will I?"

"That's true. How do you feel about leaving the planet, even if it is only for a few days?"

"Actually, I've never left the planet's surface since I arrived here as a young man, accompanied by my bride. In fact, we were the first couple to work the soil of this planet, once the terra forming was completed and Nivarna 7 was designated ready for habitation."

"If that's the case, don't you think that you're due a break? I'm sure that you'll make your presence felt at the system-wide gathering and, after all, you're better qualified to speak about your future than anyone else. I've always felt that you would make an excellent public speaker. So don't hold back, it's your fellow farmers that you'll be speaking to; tell them how you feel."

The two friends sat on the verandah, chatting, until the sun finally set behind the horizon and it was time to get some sleep.

The area around the spaceport on Nivarna 1, was buzzing with activity. There were only two days to go before all the delegates for the system-wide meeting began to arrive. There couldn't have been a better location chosen for such a gathering, as Nivarna 1 was equipped with a restaurant and facilities to accommodate the delegates overnight. These amenities were not included when the remainder of the system was developed. The reason given? To save money, as usual. The restaurant and sleeping facilities had been 'metabolised', as there wasn't any call for them normally, but this meeting was an exceptional occasion and the delegates would need to be cared for.

The first group to arrive were from Nivarna 9 and they were ushered through the procedures that every visitor was required to submit to and then were directed into the bar. Over the next few hours the delegates from the other planets arrived and the volume of the voices, as they greeted one another, increased as each group joined in. In many instances they were able to meet those they spoke to over the inter-planetary communications system, but had never met. By mid-day, Nivarna 1 time, all of the delegates had arrived, their baggage had been dispersed to their allocated rooms and they were ready for the meal that had been prepared for them.

After they had enjoyed their meal, they all assembled in the meeting hall and were asked to sit in the area assigned for each planet. This arrangement would enable the counting of votes cast by each planet's delegates, when decisions had to be made. As they awaited the start of proceedings there was a feeling of excited expectation, as they all wanted to see Hamish Hamilton in real life. Would he fulfil their expectations? They all thought about members of each planet's farming community, who had lost their lives, as a result of the many unexplained happenings that had taken place on each planet and felt a resentment towards Earth, due to its lack of reaction and assistance. Many felt that this was the time to make their feelings known and teach Earth a lesson it wouldn't forget.

As the hall's clock approached the due time for the session to commence, a hush slowly descended over the audience. Some of them were feeling drowsy, following the meal and the early start, by their planetary time, that they had made. Right on time, a man walked out onto the stage. His appearance was met by generous applause, accompanied by a variety of mental questions: "Who's this?" "Is this Hamish?"

"When will we hear from the top man?" and many other similar questions.

"Good afternoon all," he said. "I'm Hamish's assistant and I'm here to welcome you all and to introduce the planned sequence of events for the next couple of days. After we've been through all of that, Hamish will take over this spot to introduce his feelings on the subject of the lack of support from Earth, to assist us in coping with many unusual incidents that have beset us all." He continued speaking for a while, but always kept an eye on the clock, as they had realised the psychology of the regular changing of the speaker, to keep the audience interested. He concluded his section by saying, "...and now, I'm pleased to announce our keynote speaker, Hamish Hamilton!"

The two of them patted each other on the back, as they passed on the edge of the stage, not hearing the varied forms of welcome that were being made in conjunction with Hamish's arrival.

"Good afternoon friends, fellow farmers!"

The audience responded with a very loud, "Good afternoon."

Hamish smiled and then settled into the speech that he had been preparing for weeks. He knew it off by heart, although he still took his notes with him just in case his memory failed him at any time. He berated Earth for its lack of action in coming to their aid, in a time of trouble when members of the farms on each planet were losing their lives, due to the unexplained incidents and events. "Our next speaker will explain to you all, the similar things that have been taking place on Earth, although in most situations they've been hushed up, never making it onto the broadcast news programmes or the news media. So you'll be learning things that Earth's population isn't aware of." The speech continued, slowly increasing in force and intensity to the point where cries of "Yeah!" and "That's it!" were being spontaneously shouted from the audience.

This reached its climax when Hamish started to demand action against Earth, in retaliation to their treatment of the Nivarna planets. "We have to take action and show them how we feel!" the final syllable being accompanied by a judicious number of fist bangs on the podium. As the final words passed out of his mouth, he took two steps back and raised both of his arms. The audience cheered and gave him a standing ovation, not noticing his somewhat laboured walk off of the stage.

Once he'd arrived in the wings, out of sight of the audience, he slumped down in a chair.

"You all right, Hamish?" his assistant asked.

"I'm not feeling too good at the moment. I think I'll go and lay down, until I have to go on again."

"I didn't think there was the usual fire in the conclusion of your speech, as there was when you rehearsed in your office. It'll be the afternoon break in a little while. Would you like a sandwich along with a coffee, to give you a boost before you go back on?"

"That would fit the bill, thank you. I'll go and lay down now – see you in a minute."

As the speaker related the various incidents that had taken place on Earth, he was surprised by the reaction of the audience. Rather than expressions of shock, accompanied by sharp intakes of breath, he was receiving cheers and applause; the more extreme the incident, the louder the reaction. It seemed that rather than feeling sorry for the home population, it was more like they were pleased that it was happening to them as well. At least I'm entertaining them, he thought to himself, as he continued to present his material. Finally, he was able to thank the audience for their attention, which elicited another voluminous cheer and then he announced the break for a drink.

"I've never been so ready to exit a stage as I am now," he said the moment he returned to the safety of the wings. "The material received the reverse to what I expected, which came as a shock. I never thought they would react that way. Anyway, I'm ready for a sit down and a cup of tea."

"What about a wet flannel across your forehead?" asked one of the stagehands.

"Not a bad idea," he replied, "not a bad idea."

Hamish's assistant, Bert, knocked on his door and awaited a reply. He was called into the room and greeted by a revived Hamish. He looked much brighter having lost the pale look he had had when he came off the stage. He appeared to have a rosy glow now, which matched his fresh white shirt, along with a new tie.

"My word," Bert exclaimed. "We do look better now, don't we?"

"I'm glad you approve," Hamish replied. "Let's get going. This is the most important speech of the whole gathering. I've got to put it over in the very best way I can. I want it to be a memorable occasion. It's what we've been working for all this time. Then it's all in their hands when they vote on the best course of action to take."

The two friends stood waiting in the wings.

"Are you ready?" Bert asked Hamish.

"As ready as I'll ever be," he replied.

Bert walked out onto the stage and asked over the intercom if everyone could gather back in the meeting room, adding that the last speech of the day would commence in ten minutes.

Hamish walked onto the stage and stood behind the podium, as he was warmly greeted by the audience. He started to relate his main speech, one that Bert had heard so many times before as they wrote and adjusted it. Everything was going well, but then Hamish began to stumble over his words. He had a drink from the glass of water on the podium. Bert was worried now. The drink was their signal that something wasn't right. Then Hamish stopped mid-sentence, started again, for few sentences and then stopped completely. Those in the front rows of the audience and those watching from the wings, could see that Hamish was gripping the podium so tightly that his knuckles had turned white. The hall was as silent as it was possible for it to be. Hamish's fingers were unable to grip any longer and he fell to the floor, the sound echoing around the silent hall.

Bert rushed onto the stage, felt for a pulse in Hamish's neck and then called for the medics. He took off his jacket and laid it over Hamish and then stepped over to the microphone.

"Could you all please return to the restaurant, while we get the situation resolved. We're unable to close the curtains as we are in front of them and we need a little privacy for Hamish. Thank you." He then turned back to assist his friend, as the delegates filed silently out of the hall and the curtained doors were closed behind them.

The medics quickly got to work, using their diagnostic equipment to determine the cause of the problem. Using a portable scanner they were able to ascertain that Hamish had experienced a major stroke and his body had shut down, temporarily. He was placed on a stretcher and carried outside to the medics' vehicle, which contained a stasis chamber, which would stop any further deterioration until he arrived at the medical facility. Hamish was then whisked away, leaving Bert to pick up the pieces and present the remainder of Hamish's speech.

A couple of nosey delegates peeked through the doors into the main hall and when they noticed that the stage was clear, they made their way back to their seats. It didn't take long for the others to notice, so they began to drift back into the hall as well. By the time that Bert appeared in the wings, all psyched up to deliver the remainder of the speech, his audience was already sitting quietly in the hall awaiting his arrival. As he walked out onto the stage and headed for the podium, he was warmly greeted by the audience.

"I'm sure you'll like to know what's happening with Hamish?"

This statement elicited a positive response from the audience, who were rather shocked by seeing the main speaker, the man they had come to listen to, collapse on the stage in front of them. They'd all seen many unusual things in their time, but seeing Hamish collapse the way he did, had shocked many of them more than they would have expected.

"I can't say that Hamish is out of the woods just yet; in fact it will probably take him some time to regain some form of normality. You see, the medics seem to think that he had a massive stroke, which accounts for the way he reacted. He actually said that he felt unwell following his first speech today, although we felt that it was due to exhaustion, caused by all the work he had been doing to be ready for this gathering. Anyhow, the hospital will keep us up to date with his progress and I'm sure that you'll join with me in sending him our best wishes." This statement resulted in a loud, positive response from the audience.

As the applause began to die down, he stepped forward to the podium. “Thank you. I’m sure Hamish would appreciate that. Anyway, to the matter in hand. I should have introduced myself to you before now, but the need didn’t arise. I’m Bert Duckworth and I’ve worked on this project with Hamish for a couple of years now, both of us feeling that we needed to show Earth, in no uncertain way, how we feel about our situation. The plan is for me to deliver the remainder of the speech that Hamish was giving when he was taken ill. I hope I’ll do it justice...” At this point the applause started again, drowning out the remainder of statement, “... it’s best that I present it, as I helped to write it, in the first place.”

Once again, he waited for the applause to die down and then he began to deliver the speech from the paragraph that Hamish concluded with. Towards the end of the speech, the various ways the Nivarna planets could demonstrate their feelings about Earth’s lack of assistance were discussed along with the possible reactions that could be instigated by the Earth authorities. Overall, it was felt that the best action would be for all twelve planets to stop sending their supplies to Earth, as they currently did. If that was the decision reached they had to plan how they would deal with Earth’s response.

At this point, two stagehands carried out another podium and set it up in front of the stage, level with the first row of the audience.

“As this situation is going to affect us all,” Bert said, “it would be a good time to get your feelings on the various points that we’ve discussed so far.”

Members of the audience began to move towards the central gap between the chairs and to queue up, waiting to make their point or suggestion. When he saw how the length of the queue was building up, he quickly resolved how to limit the number of speakers. “I think that to limit the time this exercise will take, if someone relates a suggestion that you were going to make, could you please leave the queue and sit down again, otherwise we’ll all be here until midnight.”

The scheme worked successfully, with the queue losing a quarter of its length by the time the first two speakers had made their points. The third speaker stepped up to the microphone. "If we decide that all twelve planets act together, which seems to be the most sensible course of action we can take," he paused while the approving noises died down, "the Earth is likely to use its force to set up a blockade to prevent us receiving any supplies. So we need to ensure that we have the facilities for the planets, as a group, to become self-sufficient. To enable us to be ready, I suggest that we take a few weeks to prepare, by gathering all we need, before announcing our proposed course of action."

The moment the last word had passed his lips, the building erupted with applause and the remainder of the queue dwindled to just a couple of speakers. Although the last couple of speakers were given their chance to speak, they didn't add anything of substance to the discussion.

Bert stepped forward to the microphone once again. "I feel that we're ready now, to take a decision on our course of action. First of all, we'll ask for a show of hands to approve, or disapprove, the various courses of action proposed and then there will be an official ballot box decision made by the official delegates from each planet. The result of the show of hands will, of course, be instant, whereas the ballot box decision will be announced tomorrow morning. We have to do it this way, in case we're accused of basing our course of action on a show of hands made by a chosen group of people. Everything has to be done legally. Earth authorities will use every trick in the book to undermine us and turn Earth's population against us, which won't do them any good, as they'll soon realise when food supplies dry up. Let's now have your applause for the various proposed courses of action!"

Each of the proposed choices was announced in turn and a sound-level meter used to measure the volume of the applause. There were other more sophisticated and accurate methods available, but a sound meter was the cheapest option. The meter wasn't really required, as the proposal made by the speaker from Nivarna 7, was way above all of the rest.

"I think that the audience's choice is quite clear. Discuss your choice with your delegates and they have until nine this evening to place their ballot sheets in the box, here." He pointed at a box on a small table in front of the stage. "The box will be guarded to prevent any adjusting of the result. So that's it for today. Enjoy your evening meal and get a good night's rest and I'll see you all in the morning."

As they began to drift in for breakfast the next morning, they noticed a change in the overall feeling of those serving them. They were still pleasant enough, but there was an underlying change, although undetermined, that seemed to be hanging over every staff member that they met. This became the main topic of conversation when they all met together in the main hall for the ballot result and final session of the gathering.

A middle-aged lady walked onto the stage and stopped at the podium. "Good morning everyone," she said. "I'm sorry that Bert isn't here to welcome you this morning, but he only returned from the hospital a short time ago, having been at Hamish's bedside all night. So I hope I'll do."

"You'll do for me, love," came from the back of the hall and was then accompanied by a wolf-whistle from elsewhere in the audience.

"Thank you, for your kindly welcome. I only wish that I was here under better circumstances. I'm sorry that I bring you sad news. Hamish died at approximately three-thirty, our time, this morning, the doctors having done all that they could for him. As you can imagine, all the plans that were made to make this a happy gathering for you all, have been somewhat disrupted. Before we continue on with the business that we gathered together to discuss, I think that it would be proper if we held a minutes silence now, to show our respect not only for Hamish, but also for those who have lost their lives in this strange situation that we're in."

Once the minute was concluded, Lara, for that was the lady's name, announced the result of the ballot box vote.

"I'm sure that it will be no surprise for you when I tell you that all the ballots were for every planet to withhold all further supplies of food to Earth. We will officially make the statement announcing our planned course of action on the first of the month after next. This announcement triggered enthusiastic applause from the audience, which lasted a good few minutes. When it finally subsided, Lara continued. “This gives us all approximately six weeks to ensure that we are ready to become self-sufficient, then we’ll have to start to work together, enabling us all to survive, when the Earth authorities show their true colours. Good luck to you all!”

CHAPTER 12

NEW HORIZONS

The conversation continued as they left the dining hall and made their way back to the main meeting area.

"I should rejoin the rest of the lab technicians, otherwise my absence will raise more questions. Whatever is said to us this afternoon, try to read between the lines, then you might be able to discern the true story. Just be careful. I've had a feeling ever since I arrived here, that we're under surveillance. Watch what you do and say. I hope to see you later."

They watched as Chris walked down the hall to sit in the section occupied by the lab technicians.

"He's a canny fellow, that one," Doug said. "I'd never considered the point of surveillance. Do you think it carries any weight?"

Stephen thought about the question for a moment and then said, "It certainly would fit in with the unusual pattern of this operation. There's something else that's been in my thoughts. Is he for real, or is he a plant?" The two of them sat in contemplation for a few moments, before either of them spoke. Stephen continued. "As I've had more experience of this kind of thing than you will have had. I suggest we watch how he interacts with the other technicians. It won't be conclusive, but may point us in the right direction."

As they sat near the back of the hall, they had a reasonably clear view of what was taking place in front of them. Watching him interact with those around him, they felt that Chris was behaving quite normally and they were actually being paranoid. "After all," said Doug, "what would they gain by placing a plant in amongst us all. I think we're over-reacting. Because of our history, we've become suspicious of anyone who shows fellow feeling."

"I do believe that you're right," replied Stephen. "We need to..." he stopped then, as the chairman walked onto the platform and signalled for silence.

"Good afternoon everyone. Did you enjoy your lunch?" There was muffled response from the audience, which he assumed to be in the affirmative. "This afternoon," he continued, "a different speaker will shine some light on what this is all about and the project that you've all been selected for." He exited the platform, his place being taken by a tall, older man, wearing a khaki uniform and a cap.

"As expected, this is a military operation," Doug exclaimed.

"Have you noticed," Stephen replied, "his uniform hasn't any badges or insignia. There's no way that he can be identified, or who he represents!"

"At least we can tell that he's a military man, just from the way he carries himself."

"But where in the military? That organisation is like the roots of a tree. There are many departments and offshoots, many of which are not known about and want to remain that way."

"So what you're saying is, that he could actually be anybody, just a person, who happens to be dressed in a military uniform?"

"Well, he wasn't introduced by name, was he? Anyway, let's see what he has to say for himself."

He'd already started speaking by the time their conversation concluded, although they hadn't missed anything of any importance, as it was obvious why he had been chosen for this particular assignment. He had the ability to be able to speak for five minutes, without actually saying anything of any merit and was able to continue in the same vein for as long as required. He had what was once labelled an 'upper class' accent, even though those once thought to be upper class were assimilated into the general population a long while ago. Well, that's what people in the general population believed. Those of the aristocracy of old had fought too long and hard to give up their position and influence, so things carried on as normal, although under a cloak of acceptability. No titles were ever used any more, except within families and the ancient Office of Heraldry when performing their functions.

As they expected, the speech started with a fair amount of waffle and flannel not really saying anything at all, although it eventually began to convey some points of real interest.

"As it now takes so long for us to get to the outer planets of the Nivarna group, it was felt that a new improved propulsion system was needed for our ships." This sounded quite plausible, whereas it actually was a well thought out cover story.

The Earth knew that it was under attack by an unknown enemy, the cause of hostilities had not been ascertained, although Earth along with all of the Nivarna planets had felt the brunt of the attacks. They were developing this new engine for military purposes, to better prepare them for retaliatory attacks on their enemies, once they had determined who they were!

He was coming towards the end of his speech now. "So members of various services have been indirectly working on this project, or have been assigned to it, because of their skills..."

Stephen whispered, "Or because they're nosey so and so's," into Doug's ear, causing a smile to appear on his somewhat dour face.

"...Will make up the crew of this experimental craft. The final crew listing will be determined over the next few days, while you are all instructed about the craft that you could be crewing. Although at this time the information you will receive will not be of a sensitive nature, especially as some of you will be designated to other duties. I can tell you that the small military force that has been assigned to this project..."

Stephen was elbowed in the ribs by Doug.

"...Along with the medical team..."

Stephen reciprocated Doug's action.

"... Will definitely be crew members and as such will be receiving space transport training in the near future, while others will be sent for specialist training."

The speech continued for a while longer, without revealing anything else of any substance. When it had concluded, it was time for the afternoon break and, as expected, Chris joined them to discuss the proceedings.

"What do you make of all that?" he asked, telling them that he'd nicknamed the speaker 'The Unknown Soldier', due to his lack of insignia and name. Both Stephen and Douglas thought that it was an excellent name for him, deciding to use it themselves when speaking about him.

"So you two are to become spacemen. I presume one is going to be Kirk and the other Spock," he said, using names from an ancient space show, names that everyone seemed to know.

"Actually," Stephen replied, "it would be more accurate if I was Kirk and Doug was Bones," demonstrating his knowledge of the same show.

Doug was bewildered by all of this, as he'd never paid any attention to old fictional space shows when he was younger. Although he didn't want to show it, he was rather apprehensive about going into space. He wasn't even that keen on flying, he preferred to keep his feet on solid ground. He didn't appear to have much choice now, it seemed that the die was cast and he was to become the medical officer on a spacecraft, an experimental one at that. He cast his eyes at Stephen and Chris, who seemed excited by the prospect of being blasted up into the heavens, to face who knows what. He began to wonder, would they survive? What would happen if this new craft failed? Could they get lost? Doug didn't sleep very well that night. He kept having dreams consisting of floating alone in space, without any chance of rescue, or survival.

While Stephen was getting ready for breakfast the next morning, Douglas was sitting on the end of his bed bemoaning his lack of sleep, which was exacerbated by a rather dramatic thunderstorm that raced over the camp during the night, the lightning strike illuminating the room momentarily, even though the curtains were closed. As he awaited his turn in the bathroom, the TV was on, relaying the morning's news. Doug wasn't paying much attention to the programme, until he saw an image that he recognised. "Steve! Steve!"

"What is it?" Stephen replied.

"Come and look at this. Our old base is on the news," Douglas explained.

Steve wandered into the room, bath towel wrapped around his middle and shaving foam on his face. There were more modern ways of shaving, but Steve preferred using a razor and foam. He settled on the end of his bed, just after the story had commenced.

"We brought this story to you yesterday afternoon, not long after it had happened. But then the authorities closed the story down and have only released the full information to us now, so that we can bring you the story as accurately as possible," the reported said, clarifying the reason for the delay,

"Must be something serious, if they did that," Steve responded.

"That's what I was thinking," Doug replied.

Somehow, the reporter had managed to gain access to the base and was allowed to show the viewers where the incident had taken place. Accompanying her was the base commander who answered the questions she put to him as they walked together.

"The base was being inspected by Major General Sir Charles Deadwood," the reporter stated.

"Very aptly named," quipped Stephen, as Doug chuckled under his breath.

"Everything had gone to plan, until the inspection reached this point, the medical section," she stated.

"I notice that your name's been removed from the plaque outside. They obviously don't expect you back!" Stephen said.

Douglas didn't reply.

Steve's statement reinforced his worries about space flight and cemented his concerns about surviving the whole experience, although watching the report did help to distract his thought patterns.

Speaking directly to camera, she continued her report. "The incident took place in the isolation ward, where there was only one patient."

"And we both know who that is, don't we?" Doug pointed out.

"Yes, that's the locksmith whose injuries were caused by an unknown form of radiation, on that aborted attempt to determine the contents of an apparently disused warehouse in Northumberland," was Steve's reply.

"The poor man was slowly dying in a most painful way," Doug explained.

They were directly involved with the situation that was

developing before their eyes, so they both fell silent, watching closely as the story unravelled.

The reported picked up the thread again. "The inspection team were required to wear anti-radiation suits, because of the condition of the patient. As they approached the patient's bed, he slowly, very slowly turned his head to look at them and they were surprised by the extent that the radiation had ravaged his features. The patient's doctor walked over to him and introduced the visiting party. Once they saw the doctor standing by his bed, they moved in somewhat closer, as up to this point they had stayed well back. What exactly occurred next the doctor wasn't too sure, as it all happened so quickly. I shall relate to you, therefore, what the doctor told me. The Major General leant forward over the patient's bed and asked him how he felt. The doctor had to intervene and explain that the patient was unable to reply, as it was too painful for him to try and do so. While this was taking place, there was a bright flash, coupled with a loud bang, from underneath the sheets, at the patient's midriff. The Major General fell backwards, his hands clutching his chest, with blood pumping from between his fingers. While all eyes were watching this scenario, the patient managed to swivel the gun around and another shot rang out, taking the life of the patient."

Steve and Doug were stunned. Doug was the first to speak.

"On a number of occasions, Ken – that's the locksmith's name – had said to me that he was sure that those higher up the food-chain knew exactly what was going on, but omitted to warn us before we went on the mission, which ended up with him in his current condition. He was determined to get his own back before he died and it appears that he fulfilled his desires."

While Doug had been speaking, the reporter was reviewing the information they had on the deceased and this was visually backed up with any photos that they were able to lay their hands on, coupled with long, lingering shots of the ward in which the incident took place. She then picked up the story once again, only this time from a different part of the base.

"Our investigations have revealed that neither the officer who led the operation where the patient was injured, nor the medical officer, who initially looked after the patient, are no longer serving on this base. When we tried to find out where they had gone, the base commander informed us that even he didn't know. All he did know was that they both had been given special orders that transferred them to an unknown location. If anything else is uncovered, we'll let you know as soon as possible but for now, back to the studio."

By the time that they arrived in the restaurant, breakfast was well under way. They continued to discuss and speculate about the TV report.

"He must have planned this, over a period of time," Doug surmised. "He had to wait until an official was in the offing and then somehow managed to obtain the pistol he used."

"He wouldn't have been able to keep it in the bed with him, would he?" Stephen queried.

"That's what I was wondering about," Doug replied. "He must have had an accomplice, who brought it into him on the day a visit was due to occur."

"Whoever it was, he obviously had access to a weapon, which isn't as easy as you would think on a military base and he also had access to the medical section so that he would be able to deliver the weapon to Ken, on the appropriate day."

"There's much more to this than we know. It's all rather confusing," was Doug's response.

A few moments later, when a seat opposite them became available, Chris quietly took up occupancy. "Morning, gents. Just before you appeared there was an announcement, one which will most likely affect the both of you."

"Come on then," Stephen said rather abruptly, "tell us more. You can't leave it there."

A rather startled Chris said, "I didn't intend to just leave it like that. The person who made the announcement stated that..."

At that moment an officer strode into the room and raising his voice he said, "Ladies and gentlemen, could you please give me your attention for a few moments. The personnel that have been selected for space orientation have been chosen and a list will be placed on the notice-board outside the lecture hall. Please check to see if you are included in this group. If you are, please use the morning to pack your possessions. If not, please meet in the lecture hall as normal. Thank you for your attention."

"Do you want to have a look at the list?" Doug asked.

"Before I find out what they intend to do with me now, I'm going to take my time and enjoy what could be my last mug of decent coffee, for who knows how long. If they want me sooner, they'll come and collect me," was Stephen's reply.

The other two agreed that that was excellent thinking, joining him in one more mug of coffee.

CHAPTER 13

A WORRYING DEVELOPMENT

The Nivarna 12 delegates returned to a planet in turmoil; one that had a history of seismic activity, so the geologists said, although there hadn't been much activity in the past few thousand years. It was obvious from the make-up of the soil that it had at one time been very active volcanically. The farmers were now benefiting from a soil that contained high levels of minerals and nutrients that helped them grow bumper crops.

Because of the planet's history, a seismology station had been commissioned before the humans had ever moved in and forged a farming community. The day following the departure of the delegates to the system-wide meeting, the planet was woken by the sound of alarms, emanating from the seismic station. There had been one similar occurrence some years before, although that was a false alarm. This time it most certainly wasn't. A couple of cracks in the planet's surface had appeared in the middle of a farmer's field, each one expelling a small amount of toffee-like lava, along with a clear, odourless gas that was to cause some unexpected results.

Slowly, but surely, the planet's previous state began to reassert itself, having been dormant for many years. The surface cracks were the first signs of the impending problems that they all would have to deal with. Evidence began to accumulate in the site where the first cracks appeared. Now they had spread and joined together at a central point. It took less than 24 hours for a tell-tale cone of dust and ash to accumulate at this central point and continued to grow during the following days.

Technicians from the seismology station were dispatched to the site, to place measuring probes around the area before it grew any larger and they were unable to gain further access. It was too far from their base to run cables all the way back, so they set up a radio transmitting hub approximately 150 yards from the cone. This was the longest cable run that they had available, without employing extension connections. Any joins in the cable could interrupt the connection if any violent seismic activity took place. Once it was all set up, a test signal was sent back to base to ensure that the circuit was functioning correctly. The moment the signals from the various probes were put on line, the indicators at the base were off the scale and the geophysicists had to turn the sensitivity down so a reading could be obtained.

The two technicians had been breathing in the undetectable gas for well over an hour now and it was beginning to have an effect. They had worked together for many years on a variety of assignments and had always got on well. But on their journey back to the seismic station, they started to snap at one another. Disagreements followed, each growing in intensity until they finally began to assault one another. This wasn't lightweight bickering, this was a no-holds-barred fight: blood was drawn and a couple of teeth were knocked out.

The team leader called them on the communicator to ask about their progress, but was unable to get a response, which wasn't surprising, as they were too busy fighting to pay attention to a bleeping communicator. Two of the base's security staff were assigned to go and investigate the situation. Because they didn't know what they'd find, it was suggested that they use two transport pods, just in case either one of the technicians was hurt and required evacuating in the prone position.

As they drew close to the site they couldn't believe what they saw. There were the two technicians, who had been the best of friends for as long as anyone could remember, rolling about on the ground, trading blows with one another. By the time they'd managed to pull them apart, the rescue team were as bloodied as the fighters were. A four-way altercation developed, with the security guards dragged into the conflict, although that only lasted for a few moments, until the well aimed right hooks from the security guards eventually brought hostilities to a conclusion.

One of the protagonists was placed in the rear seat of each of the transport pods and strapped securely in place. This proved much simpler with the fighters in an unconscious state and would have been a more difficult task if arms and legs had been flailing about. As it was, the journey back to the base was trouble-free, although their passengers were beginning to stir by the time the pods stopped outside the base.

For safety's sake, they removed them one at a time and soon realised that the reason the two of them were fighting was because there wasn't anyone else around. The moment the seat straps were removed, the security guards became the target of choice, although the level of violence seemed to be decreasing in intensity. The two technicians were placed in two separate side rooms and affixed to chairs by the judicious use of heavy-duty sticky tape.

The seismic team leader, Professor André Lagardé, contacted the space port, which was only a short distance away and requested a medical team, to deal with the various injuries sustained during the skirmish. He also asked them to bring two oxygen cylinders, along with the appropriate face masks. The request for the oxygen prompted a question from Dr Janice Fielding, one of the station's two geophysicists.

"What are the oxygen cylinders for? They don't seem to be having any problems with their breathing?" she asked.

The professor turned to her and explained. "On earth, some years ago, I was investigating some volcanic vents that had opened up in the fields alongside a village in a volcanic area of South America. At that time I noticed a similar incident to the one we've all experienced today. Those that had been tending their crops closest to the vents, began to act in a very aggressive manner. Almost immediately this developed into all-out fighting, involving both men and women. The only way we managed to calm them down, was to have them breath in some pure oxygen, for a short period of time, which seemed to counteract the gas that they'd obviously inhaled."

When the medical team arrived, the lead nurse saw the state of the two security men and asked them what they'd been involved in. The most vocal of the two replied, "Don't worry about us, you should see the state of the other two!"

"Oh, it's like that is it," she replied. The professor then entered into the conversation and explained the whole situation.

"I've never heard of that before," another member of the

medical team exclaimed.

"Neither have I. In all my years of nursing I've never had to deal with anything along those lines before. But if we can avoid having to deal with aggressive patients, by giving them some oxygen, I'm all for it. Let's take a look at them."

The nurse, along with the professor and the security men, entered each of the two side rooms in turn to assess the current state of the two technicians.

The seismology and medical teams gathered in the central area to decide upon a course of action. It was decided that they would treat the two security men, while the two technicians had their dose of oxygen. Hopefully by the time the security men were patched up, the other two would be safe enough to be released from their chairs so they could be treated, although the security staff would be on hand, just in case remnants of the aggressive behaviour returned.

The medical team were highly efficient, applying the needed soothing treatment to the wounds and making their patients as comfortable as they could be. The two technicians would both need to see a dentist and arrange to have implants fitted, to replace their missing teeth. About an hour after their arrival, the medical team left the base and suggested that anyone venturing near to volcanic vents wore breathing equipment in future. The seismology team heartily agreed with the suggestion, after seeing the effect the vent gas had had on their colleagues.

Things slowly returned to normal, although it was a couple of weeks before the technicians and the security men were able to remove the plasters from their faces. The vents carried on spreading and the cone continued to grow. The team also noticed an increase in seismic activity from their instruments, that had been placed all over the planet. Although no one voiced their fears, they were all very concerned about the way things were developing and had begun to worry about the future of the planet.

A couple of days later the professor received a communication from Earth, which had been sent detailed reports of what was taking place, informing him that two more staff members were on their way and would be joining them in the next couple of days. This information was well received by the team, who felt that the way the situation seemed to be developing, their team of five would struggle to cope with the demands being placed upon them.

A few days later, the most seismically active period that any of them had experienced on Nivarna 12, took place. Following this activity, the professor gathered them all together to give each one of them an opportunity to expound their feelings and theories concerning the situation that was developing and to speculate on what they thought it meant for the planet's future. An honest discussion followed, with every team member feeling free to express themselves. The overall feeling was that if the current situation continued to expand, the future for the planet didn't seem particularly positive.

Professor Lagardé, accompanied by Chris and Janice Fielding, the two geophysicists, were waiting at the space port for the arrival of their two new team members. Although nothing was actually said, they all felt that this additional manpower and expertise could well be the required stimulus leading to a turning point in their deliberations concerning the future of the planet.

An announcement blared out from the PA system: "The passengers and crew from the transport, have now disembarked." The three of them removed themselves from their seats by the panoramic windows and made their way to greet their guests. It didn't take a great deal of effort to pick them out, as they were both dressed in the garish clothes that were the current trend on Earth. The professor stepped towards them, stretched out his hand and shook hands with each of them in turn.

"Welcome to Nivarna 12," the professor said in greeting. "I'm Professor Lagardé and my companions are Chris and Janice Fielding, the unit's geophysicists. We were told that two extra team members would be joining us, but weren't informed who they would be, so we don't know what your names are. Would you tell us, please?"

"Sorry about that," the woman said, in a heavily accented voice, "I'm Ulana Litarpenko."

"And I'm Ian Stuart," the man said in a broad Scottish accent.

“Welcome to you both,” the professor replied. “Would you like something hot to eat, along with a hot drink? I know travelling in a transport isn’t too comfortable, although the crew do the best they can.”

“That would be marvellous,” Ian said.

“That’s just what I need,” echoed Ulana.

Sitting at a table that would accommodate them all in the bar-cum-restaurant, they noticed that Ulana was making a thorough check on her surroundings, even looking under the table.

“Don’t worry,” Chris said, “there aren’t any hidden microphones here.”

“Sorry about my caution,” she replied. “We’re all so used to being under surveillance back on Earth, that you think that everywhere else is the same. So I presume that it’s safe to speak openly here?”

“Perfectly safe,” Janice replied.

“I won’t go into details now, for that I’ll wait until we’re all assembled in the Seismology Centre, but I will tell you that once I knew I was being sent here, I did some digging around and uncovered some documents that appear to explain our current situation. It was too dangerous to remove the originals, so I brought copies of them all with me. Then you’ll know why you’re suffering all of this seismic activity.”

At that point the waiter arrived with the food, so that was the end of the matter until they returned to base.

CHAPTER 14

TRUE COLOURS

In the time that had passed since the system-wide gathering, the team on Nivarna 1, now without Hamish since his recent demise, had been busy drawing up the formal Declaration of Intent to be sent to Earth. When a format that was acceptable to everyone was agreed, a copy of this document was transmitted to each of the Nivarna planets. When a positive response was received from all the delegates, the declaration was drawn up in a legally-acceptable format and then forwarded to each of the Nivarna planets for their delegates to add their signature.

Following the return of the fully signed declaration to Nivarna 1, Earth was contacted. A meeting was arranged with the re-established Nivarna Operating Committee, and the three delegates who represented all of the Nivarna planets. No indication was given for the purpose of the meeting, although the committee members had a feeling that they weren't going to like what they would hear.

Volunteers for the trip to Earth were few in number. They all realised what could happen when the declaration was read to the committee. They didn't know it, but plans had been put in place to ensure the delegates' safe return. Eventually, eight volunteers came forward and as they hailed from different planets, a gathering was arranged for them all on Nivarna 1. During the gathering the possibilities of their mission were explained to them in no uncertain terms. After hearing this, three of them decided that it wasn't for them after all. They were thanked for volunteering and then returned home. At least they made some new friends. The five that were left were a dedicated bunch and were finally divided into a team of three delegates and two back-ups, in case of illness or accident taking one of the delegates out of the picture.

It was the day of the trip to Earth and the transport craft was in orbit, waiting for their arrival. Just before they entered the anti-grav craft that would take them to the waiting transport, they were informed about the rescue plan that would take place if required. It was essential to leave it until this late stage, to protect those who were involved in putting the plan into action. If they were uncovered, by one word or comment in the wrong place, their lives would be in danger.

The trip to Earth was uneventful, although the crew did seem to be on edge. The pilot explained the reason. "The majority of transport crews are on edge these days, following the Transport 113 incident. They're all worried that something similar could happen to them. So it's quite understandable, under the circumstances. The sooner Earth sorts the situation out the better and it won't be a day too soon as far as the transport crews are concerned," the pilot stated.

The delegates began to wonder about the effect that their mission might have. Would Earth's lack of interest and concern towards the Nivarna planets change, once they realised how much they actually relied on them? Or would it make matters worse? No one voiced an opinion, although they personally couldn't foresee a positive outcome. The more they thought about it, the more they began to worry about their own personal safety.

"At least we have the escape plan in place."

"That's if it works as planned."

"If we carry on like this, we won't complete the job entrusted to us. Just remember, the population of twelve planets are relying on the three of us to do as we promised. Do you want to let them down? I don't."

As the anti-grav craft descended towards the surface of the Earth, all three delegates wondered about the kind of reception they would receive. They didn't need to worry, as they received a most cordial reception from the group of officers who were there to meet them. They were conveyed into the city in the plushest car that any of the delegates had ever seen, let alone ridden in. They found the whole experience very pleasurable and intended to make the most of their visit, especially as it had been many years since any of them had visited Earth.

The car pulled up outside of what was obviously a high-class hotel and they were led inside by their guide.

“Before you get booked in, I thought it would be nice to have a meal together,” he said, “then I can explain your itinerary for the next couple of days.”

They followed him into the restaurant, feeling a little self-conscious as they walked in, as their clothes indicated to everyone that they were off-worlders. They, in turn, were rather bemused by the clothes being worn by the other diners.

“Don’t worry about them all looking at you,” the guide said, “they’re not used to seeing people from off-world, even though they’re most likely eating food that you have grown for them.”

The novelty of seeing off-worlders quickly wore off and they returned to their meals and conversations.

While they waited for their meals, their activities for the next few days were presented to them. The next day was to be taken up by a guided tour around the city, including visits to the various locations of interest and sampling some of the many kinds of food served in the city’s restaurants. The day would culminate with a cinema visit or a show in a theatre, whichever they chose. The day after that would be a free day for them to take a wander around and prepare to meet the Nirvana Operating Committee (NOC) on the following day. After this information had been presented, the delegates clarified any points they were unsure of and looked through the lists of entertainment available for them to choose from for the following evening. They hadn’t made up their minds by the time their meals arrived. If they were honest, they were somewhat overwhelmed by everything that had happened since they landed on Earth.

* * *

It was the day to meet the NOC and the delegates were feeling quite nervous. Their attitude had begun to change on their “free day to wander”. It hadn’t taken them long to realise that they were being followed. So, to prove the point, they decided to turn off the main street and into one of the many alleyways that led away from the centre of activity. They only managed a few steps into the alleyway, before they were confronted by a smartly-dressed man, who stepped out of the shadows and advised them to turn back.

"It's for your own safety," he cautioned. "There are people who frequent some of these backstreets who would rob you and possibly kill you to get what they wanted. So it's best if you stay on the main streets – okay?"

They didn't want to wander around the alleyways anyway. It was a test that proved a point; not only were they being followed, but their movements were also being tracked. There must have been a man, similar to the one who had confronted them, in each of the numerous alleyways just in case they had strayed.

They approached the meeting with the NOC, therefore, with some trepidation, now that they had a more realistic appraisal of the Earth authorities. It had taken them some time to decide which one of them would present the declaration to the committee. After a long discussion, the final choice was made by drawing straws, the one drawing the short straw having spent the previous evening reading through the declaration over and over again.

The car arrived right on time and they were whisked away into a section of the city that they hadn't visited before. This area was made up of a variety of government buildings and prestigious office complexes. The car pulled up outside a newish looking building, whereas some of the buildings in the area looked quite old and weathered, where the NOC had been moved to following the explosion at its previous premises. They were ushered into the foyer and noticed from the direction board that they were headed for the twenty-third floor, section B. The high-speed lift made short shrift of the climb, the intermediate floors flashing by at a phenomenal rate, until it slowed and stopped at floor twenty-three.

They hadn't really noticed the security staff before, even though one of them had been in the lift that they had just travelled in. But now as they sat in the foyer to the NOC's suite of offices, they realised just how many there were. They all thought back to what they had been told just before leaving

Nivarna 1. If it was required, how would a rescue take place with all of these security staff around?

Their thoughts were interrupted by a young woman, who asked them whether they would like any kind of refreshment. She looked rather surprised when they all declined her offer. She smiled and said, "If you change your mind let me know and I'll arrange it for you."

They all watched her as she walked away.

"How does she manage to walk in those shoes?"

"I was thinking more about the tightness of the skirt."

"Can you imagine her trying to do an honest day's work on any of our planets? She wouldn't last an hour."

"If she was on my planet, I don't think it would be to work in the fields!"

And so the banter continued, but it helped to defuse the tension they all felt. At least they had remembered the warning they had received concerning drinks and the like; items that could have been laced with a chemical additive. They had to keep their heads clear.

They spent their time watching the people coming and going, while making the occasional comment to one another. It was strange to think that these were the people that were involved in making decisions that affected their lives. They didn't pay much attention as a middle-aged woman walked towards them, until she stopped in front of them. "The committee is ready to see you now. Follow me, please," she announced.

This was it, the purpose of the trip was about to be fulfilled.

As they stood up, they began to feel nervous. They followed the woman past the open-plan office area and then turned into a long corridor. They had walked well over halfway along its length when the woman stopped outside a pair of imposing wooden doors. She turned and smiled at them, which was the first display of emotion that she had made.

"Don't worry, it will soon be all over and then you'll feel much better!" she said.

"I hope so," a delegate replied.

The woman opened one of the doors and stepped inside,

leaving the door open. They heard her announce their presence to the committee and then invited them in. There was no turning back now. Each of them, in turn, took a deep breath and stepped inside.

They entered a large rectangular room, with a high ceiling and two walls devoted to floor-to-ceiling windows, which flooded the room with natural light. A large part of the floor space was taken up by a highly-polished long table with rounded ends. Seven chairs were set at one end, which were occupied by the committee, with the chairman in the central position. Three more seats were set out for the delegates at the opposite end of the table. The three delegates took their places, with the delegate who would read the declaration facing the committee chairman. The woman then closed the doors and took her seat in the corner of the room, by the window, as she was to oversee the recording of the proceedings.

"Good morning all," said the chairman. "We've all met together today to pay attention to a declaration that is being presented on behalf of the Nivarna planets. First of all, the committee is interested in establishing the reasons that led to the drawing up of this declaration. Following that, we'd like to have the declaration read out to us, so a record of its contents will be included in the record of this meeting. Is everyone happy with that?"

The committee members and delegates were willing to accept the proposed arrangement. The chairman started to speak again. "Before we commence proceedings, I feel that it would be a good idea if everyone introduced themselves then we will all know who everyone is."

Following the name check, one of the delegates stood up to relate the reasons that eventually brought the declaration into existence. He spoke eloquently for approximately ten minutes, without using notes, which wasn't difficult for him as some of his associates had been involved in various incidents that had taken place. He finished his account with the destruction of Transport 113 and how it had left the transport crews feeling and included Earth's lack of response to any of these reported situations. The committee members just looked at one another and didn't say a word.

Did they know or were they kept in ignorance, the delegates wondered.

"Your lack of response, which obviously hasn't changed, is the reason that caused the idea of the declaration to come into being and then gain favour across the Nivarna system," a delegate stated.

They could see that the chairman wasn't comfortable with the way that the meeting was going, as he was shifting about his seat and beginning to get a red flush across his face. The chairman cleared his throat and then took a drink from his glass of water.

"Are you all right?" the committee member to his right asked.

"Just something in my throat," he replied.

A few of the committee members subtly smiled. They'd known the chairman for long enough to know that he was flustered and would have some awkward questions to answer once the delegates had left the room.

He cleared his throat again. "I think that it's time that we heard the declaration now, seeing that the situation that brought it into existence has been thoroughly explained to us. If there is anything else that needs to be covered before this takes place, please speak up now!"

As there wasn't a reply to his statement, it was time for the declaration to be read. The delegate in the centre chair took a sip of water from his glass and then stood up.

"Thank you Mr Chairman. Copies of this declaration will be available for all of the committee members, following the reading." He looked around and then picked up a folder that contained the declaration. He was a competent reader, who knew how to use pauses for dramatic effect, also using such occasions to look at the committee members to judge their responses. The first few paragraphs were full of legal jargon that required concentration from the reader to ensure that they were read correctly.

It wasn't until he began to cover the proposed plan of action by the Nivarna planets that reactions from the committee members started to become apparent. When the portion of the declaration stating that deliveries of food to Earth would be terminated was read out, it was as if the committee members had received an electric shock. Following this statement there was a long pause, to allow the import of the statement to sink in. A few final details were then covered, concluding the reading of the declaration. The reader almost collapsed back into his chair, the tension and pressure of the presentation having drained his system. A fellow delegate handed him a glass of water which he emptied in one continuous gulp. Slowly, he began to regain his composure.

When everything calmed down, the committee members wondered how the chairman was going to handle the situation. They could see that something was brewing as his face was beginning to look rather red again. Following a few moments of silence, he erupted into a torrent of abuse.

"Who the hell do you think you are? You're nothing but a bunch of hick farmers! The Nivarna planets were set up by Earth, for the benefit of the planets' inhabitants. So you work for us and your sole purpose is to provide food for Earth's population."

"I'm sorry that it's come to this," said a delegate, "but as we've explained, you've brought it on yourselves by not taking care of us."

While the delegate had been speaking, the chairman had depressed a button tucked under the lip of the table. A few minutes passed, the door opened and five security officers marched in.

"Take these renegades down to the cells!" the chairman barked.

The delegates were unceremoniously dragged off of their chairs and forced out of the room. They'd been expecting something like this. They were all wondering how the rescue plan was going to be able to retrieve them from such a situation.

They didn't have to worry as the plan to get them safety back to the Nivarna system was already underway.

CHAPTER 15

"THAT'S WHY WE'RE HERE!"

By the time the mugs of coffee were drained, theirs was the only table still in use. The two waitresses assigned to that dining section were sitting at a table on the other side of the restaurant and kept looking over at Doug, Stephen and Chris, to see whether they had finally finished. They were so surprised when the trio eventually stood up and were ready to leave, that they didn't move for a few seconds.

Stephen, always ready with the correct comment said to them, "We're sorry for delaying you, ladies. But we don't know when it will be that we'll get a mug of coffee that's as good as yours. Maybe we never will, so we wanted to savour what could be our last mug." As usual, his words achieved their purpose and the trio left the restaurant, leaving two happy waitresses in their wake.

Even before they reached the notice-board they knew their names would be on the list for space orientation. They were correct, so they returned to their rooms and packed their meagre possessions ready for transportation to another facility. They didn't have very long to wait. Barely fifteen minutes after completing their packing a knock on the door announced the arrival of a soldier who had been sent to collect them. They hadn't read the instructions at the bottom of the list of names. They were supposed to muster in the main foyer once they were packed. As they pushed the doors open and entered the foyer a cheer accompanied by whistling erupted from those already assembled.

The officer in charge turned to his NCO. "Is that everyone now?"

After consulting his computer the NCO replied, "Just one more to come now."

Barely a second passed before the doors burst open and a flustered looking Chris, followed by a soldier entered the foyer. He, too, was greeted by whistling and cheering. As his welcome began to subside he apologised to the officer. “I’m sorry for being late. I was delayed.”

A voice came from those already gathered. “I hope she was worth it!” which started the noise all over again.

Now that the full complement had been assembled, they were led outside to a Yamamoto personnel carrier. These vehicles were a commonplace sight on the roads these days and wouldn’t rouse any interest in those that they passed. The carrying cases containing all the personal effects were packed into the carriers, then they all climbed aboard.

The motor used in the PSV is very quiet, unlike the older engines that were still in use in some vehicles. When these quiet vehicles were first used, a number of pedestrians were knocked over because they didn’t hear the vehicle approaching. They were used to them now and made sure the road was clear before stepping out.

As the journey commenced, a few of the passengers used their personal computers to work out their route without much success. The coach stayed on the small back roads, where there wasn’t much in the way of signposts etc. So they reverted to using their GPS systems. As it was late in the day the rhythmic rocking of the coach, along with the sound of the tyres on the road, soon caused the passengers to fall asleep. Others found staring at a screen, that was moving in harmony with the movement of the coach, quite hypnotic and quickly joined those who had already fallen asleep.

Time passed by and as the coach ploughed on into the night, the passengers didn’t even notice a brief stop, while the drivers swapped over. The technology may have improved over the years, but that didn’t prevent drivers from getting tired, so relief drivers were still a necessity. Suddenly there was an almighty bang and the clouds were silhouetted against the sky. Then the rain started.

The loud noise abruptly returned a number of passengers to consciousness, as the rain hammered on the synthetic, ‘stay-clean’ glass, which had been fitted to road vehicles and trains for many years. The driver was able to see clearly as the windscreen was fitted with an ultra-sonic system that caused the glass to repel the rain and the 'stay-clean' coating prevented any smears, or dirt, compromising the driver's view. Older and vintage vehicles still used windscreen wipers, although they seemed quaint and out-of-date these days.

When the rain turned to hailstones, some of the passengers were worried that the windows would break, such was their force and size. They need not have worried. The synthetic glass that was in common use was extremely strong, having been trialled to extremes under every test that was dreamt up. The storm was spectacular, the lightning bolts shooting across the sky like some kind of alien weapon let loose upon the Earth. As the coach carried on its journey it began to leave the storm behind, although it was still raining hard when the coach turned down a driveway which led to the passengers' destination.

The coach came to a halt in a floodlit area, where a number of similar vehicles were already parked, outside a building that bore the legend B15.

"That's as close as it can get, folks," the driver announced over the intercom. "I'm afraid that you'll have to make a dash for the door!"

The passengers stirred and began to form a line along the centre of the coach. (They looked as if they were queuing up for a parachute jump.) Three of the last passengers to make a run for shelter were Stephen, Chris and Doug. Doug was halfway to the door when he slowed and stopped, while by this time the other two were taking refuge in the doorway.

"What are you doing, Doug? You'll get soaked!" shouted Stephen.

Doug continued looking at his surroundings and then made his way to the door. He explained his actions. "I stopped because this place looked very familiar. Of course it's difficult to be sure in the dark. I'll have a good look round tomorrow."

"This needs an explanation," Steve stated. "Why would this place seem familiar to you? Have you been here before?"

"A few years ago I was given an assignment as a locum at the base where military pilots and transport crews were trained and orientated. I think this is that base!"

At this juncture, Chris entered the conversation. "It makes sense, seeing that we've been sent here for similar training. Anyway, why are we standing here in the doorway, getting damp, when it's warm inside?"

As they entered the building the desire to sleep became overwhelming. Each of them presented their papers to the desk sergeant, who in turn stamped them and handed them back along with a security pass and individual room keys. As they walked away from the desk the sergeant said, "Good night, gentleman, have a good sleep." They barely acknowledged his comment, as their minds were full of the desire to sleep. Exiting the foyer they followed the signs to their individual rooms. The only comment made was by Chris. "G'night chaps. See you in the morning."

Stephen was enjoying a late breakfast and had just started on his toast when the mess hall's swing doors opened and in walked Doug. He made his way to the counter, ordered some breakfast along with a pot of coffee and then looked around, trying to locate either of his colleagues. It took a few minutes, but he eventually noticed Stephen sitting with his back to the door. He walked over to the table and had just settled into his chair, when the waitress arrived with his food. Nothing was said for the first few minutes, while Doug ate and downed the first mug of coffee of the day.

Stephen respectfully waited for a few minutes, remembering how much he'd enjoyed starting his breakfast. After about five minutes had elapsed, he spoke.

"Well, Doug, have you been here before? Last night you thought that you had. Were you right?"

While pouring a mug of coffee Doug replied. "I've had a good look round this morning and the more ground I covered, the stronger the memories became. Then I remembered. It must have been about three years ago that I came her to take the place of the camp's doctor, who had been sent on a training course. I think that I was here for about a month, it could have been longer, although I'm not really sure."

“Ten out of ten for memory,” Stephen replied. “I doubt if I could remember what I was doing three years go, let alone where I was.”

The swing doors opened again and a bleary-eyed Chris ambled over to where they were sitting. He plonked himself down in a chair, supported his head in his hands and sat there, struggling to keep his eyes open. Stephen and Doug just watched him. After a few minutes Doug commented that he thought it was amazing that someone so obviously asleep managed to find his way to the mess. Chris was totally oblivious to everything that was happening around him, although his sense of smell seemed to be operational.

“Would one of you two take pity on me and give me a mug of coffee?” he said.

“Here, have some of mine, it’s fresher than Stephen’s,” said Doug, as he poured out the steaming coffee. “Be careful, it’s very hot,” warned Doug. That didn’t seem to concern Chris at all. He gulped the dark brown liquid down his throat, as if he hadn’t had anything to drink for a week. The other two watched in amazement. It only took a couple of minutes to take effect and then it was as if a switch had been flicked on in his brain. Chris suddenly came to life.

“Time for some breakfast,” he said, as he stood up and strode off to place his order.

* * *

The course had a duration of three weeks. It bore little resemblance to the courses that trained astronauts back in the early days of space flight. Space suits were no longer required and with the advent of gravity control technology, space flight had become greatly simplified. As the trio had different functions: medical, military and technical, their individual courses tended to vary slightly. So they compared the day’s events in the mess hall, when they met together for the evening meal. In the relaxed atmosphere of the mess they were able to compare notes and learn more about each other’s function on board the ship.

It was the Friday evening at the end of the second week, when Stephen and Doug met together while they ate their evening meal.

"Have you seen anything of Chris?" Doug asked.

"I was just about to ask you the same question," Stephen replied.

They carried on their discussion concerning the day's events, as they usually did, the highlight being that some of the auxiliary nursing staff decided that this was not the kind of activity that they wanted to be involved with. The main reason being that the craft was experimental and untried. Rather than seeing it as an adventure, they chose the opposite decision. Doug's mouth opened to continue the conversation, but closed abruptly when there was a loud bang as the swing doors were forcibly opened. Through the doors came a grinning Chris sitting in an old manual wheelchair, his left leg in plaster up to the mid point of his calf.

The wheelchair was erratically guided over to the table, where Stephen and Doug moved the unnecessary chairs out of the way, so Chris was able to place the wheelchair right at the table's edge. They all settled and Doug said, "Okay, then, what have you done?"

"I was playing basketball and jumped up, attempting to persuade the ball to go through the hoop. But I landed badly and broke my ankle along with a bone in my foot. So that's my space jaunt over with!"

"You idiot!" was Stephen's compassionate contribution. "I always thought that all of this chasing around after a ball never did anyone any good."

"If that's what you think," replied Doug, "you're as big an idiot as Chris is. You'd most likely feel better if you engaged in some more exercise."

"I'm fine as I am," Stephen replied and patted his belly.

At this point Doug realised that Stephen was winding him up, so he turned his attention back to Chris. "How would you feel if I could arrange it so that you could still take part in what you call 'a space jaunt'? I have a medical reason that I've had in my mind for some time and I feel that the senior medical staff may well allow it. Leave it with me and if anyone queries your attendance at lectures, refer them to me."

"Do you really think that you can sort it out? That would be great if you could. Thanks so much," said Chris.

From the tone of his voice, Doug was able to discern that Chris really meant what he said. That response encouraged Doug to try every trick in the book, to ensure that when the ship left the Earth, all three of them would be together.

The final day of the course had arrived. The morning had been designated for the attendees to pack their personal belongings away and for those who had doubts about being involved in the flight of this experimental craft, to ask questions of those in the know, enabling them to reach a conclusion. A number of persons who were assigned for space orientation had already decided that space flight wasn't for them and had left the course.

The afternoon of the final day had been set aside for a meeting in the main hall for all those who had completed the course. The purpose was to answer some questions about the flight that hadn't been dealt with. These answers were keenly anticipated, as there were a number of items that had been omitted from their lectures and training, but were necessary for them to know.

It was an expectant crowd that gathered together that Friday afternoon. Chris was parked at the end of a row, with Stephen and Doug occupying the chairs closest to him. They received some important information that afternoon, such as details of the experimental drive for the ship. This unusual drive had been called: "The Temporal Distortion Drive", as it was designed to bend and compress space / time and shorten long journeys. The ship had been named "Explorer 1".

"That's some of the basic details about the ship, so I would now like to introduce the 'cockpit' crew to you. These three people will be in control of the ship during flight," announced the speaker. "First of all the pilot, Group Captain Ranjit Das." There was some applause as he climbed the couple of steps onto the platform and then sat down on one of the three chairs that had been set out for the flight crew.

"Secondly, the co-pilot Captain Mike Kirkwood." Once again the audience applauded as he followed his colleague and took his seat on the platform.

"Finally, as this is a complex and experimental craft, the flight engineer is a member of the design team that created this new kind of drive. May I introduce Dr Bernice Heckt." Her appearance seemed to stimulate the attention of the male members of the audience. This time the applause was louder than the previous two occasions, much to the surprise of Dr Heckt and the annoyance of the females in the audience.

"Ladies and gentleman – your flight crew," said the speaker and the applause commenced once more as the three of them stood up.

"Finally, there's one more question to be answered; one which I'm sure that you've asked yourselves. Why was I chosen for this project? You've no doubt discussed this among yourselves and noticed a similarity in your backgrounds. You have always been getting into trouble, because of asking awkward questions." A murmur rippled through the audience. "That sound which I've just heard confirms that my statement was correct. That's the reason why you were chosen. We wanted a crew that would be honest with us, one that would ask questions and maybe highlight situations we hadn't even considered. When we all meet together following the flight, we'll get an honest appraisal from you all."

The applause that followed showed the audience's approval.

"That's it for now. Please collect your personal possessions and make your way to the transport that will convey you to the space port."

CHAPTER 16

NECESSARY ADJUSTMENTS

When it was decided to send a Declaration of Intent to the Nirvana Operating Committee, it was understood that their situation was going to change. The regular supplies from Earth would cease and it was a distinct possibility that the Nivarna planets would be blockaded. Important changes would have to be made as quickly as possible.

For the first time since the inauguration of the Nivarna group, it would be necessary for one of the planets to farm livestock. Currently meat arrived frozen, although milk and eggs were in a powdered form, as they wouldn't survive the long space journey. All of the farmers that had livestock farming experience were gathered together and agreed, under the circumstances, to return to that branch of farming. Three of them were elected to travel to each of the Nivarna planets to decide which would be most suitable for rearing livestock. It was finally decided that Nivarna 11 had the most suitable climate and terrain. After some discussion, which was quite heated at times, an exchange scheme was implemented that would allow everyone time to settle into their new homes and give the livestock farmers time to build the infrastructure required for their new charges.

The volume of produce would decrease now, because the total population of all of the Nivarna planets was nowhere near the number of people they were feeding on Earth. Rather than producing a large amount of a few number of crops the agricultural planets had their crop rotations adjusted. Instead of a planet growing varieties of one particular crop, they were now producing smaller amounts of a variety of crops. Depending on planetary conditions, each farm throughout the system also planted fruit trees and bushes to produce soft fruit. They didn't have time to grow things from seedlings, so they 'obtained' these in a fully grown state and after planting, applied some newly developed chemicals that encouraged them to start producing a crop the moment they had established their root systems.

On their farm on Nivarna 7, Santos and Javan were becoming used to the new arrangements, as they were now growing a variety of crops and had introduced a farm wide crop rotation system. Like the majority of farmers, the two of them had established a fruit garden on the sunniest side of the farmhouse. Also they had set aside a small amount of land where they planted an orchard and were really looking forward to the fresh fruit, as they were currently eating canned varieties. Even though canning techniques had improved tremendously, their contents weren't as good as the real thing.

The TV feed from Earth was still operational, although they were unsure how much longer that would be the case. As had become their practice, they watched the evening news broadcast while they ate their meal. They often allowed much of the programme to wash over them, but on this particular evening one story really grabbed their attention.

"A few days ago, a delegation that represented a collusion between all of the Nivarna planets, had the cheek to state that they felt the authorities on Earth had not assisted them in dealing with some unknown outside influence that had been causing them problems. The outcome was that they threatened drastic action against Earth. There's no reason for the population of Earth to worry. The rebels that dared to meet with the Nivarna Operating Committee were given short shrift and taken off to the cells. The NOC would like to assure you all that Earth's forces will quickly quell this rebellion and return things to normal!"

Santos and Javan sat there looking at one another, Javan with a fork full of food halfway to his mouth. But that was not to be the end of the shocks for one evening. The newsreader continued.

"Now here is a message from Central Government to all Earth registered citizens who are currently residing on any of the Nivarna planets. You have one week to return to Earth and if you decline to do so, your citizenship will be revoked. In other words, you will never be allowed to return home, that's if you still call Earth home!"

Even though the news broadcast continued with the usual inanities, neither of them paid any further attention to it. In the end, Santos switched off the receiver and swivelled round in his chair so that he was facing Javan.

"Well, son, what are you going to do?"

Following the briefest of pauses, Javan said in response, "I didn't really have to give it much thought. Nivarna 7 has become home to me now, especially as you have all made me feel so welcome. Anyway, since my wife died, I no longer have anyone to return to on Earth. Why should I return there to spend life on my own and end up working in some emotionless office, when I can remain here living a healthy life with true friends all around me."

"Well said," Santos replied. "You do realise that you'll be classed as stateless, don't you?"

"So what? I'd rather be stateless than align myself with Earth, especially as I've now seen the darker side of governmental practices."

Santos was obviously thinking about something. The seed of an idea was beginning to take root in his mind. He came out of his reverie and looked straight at Javan. "The comments that were made about being stateless have given me an idea," he said. "I don't want to say anything at the moment, I'd just like to sound some others out first. If they agree with me, I'll tell you all about it."

Nothing further was said for the next few days. Then, during the evening meal Santos made an announcement. "I can tell you all about the idea that I had. It's actually being implemented as we speak."

"I realised that something was happening," Javan commented, "due to the number of visitors you were getting, along with the amount of calls you were receiving on your communicator. Can you tell me what's going on? It must be something exceptional for you to be in contact with such a large number of people!"

Santos chuckled. "You're right, of course. I wouldn't normally have contact with that many people over a year, let alone in just a few days."

"Come on then, what is it that you've kick-started?"

"Your situation started me thinking," Santos said. "Even

though the occupants of the Nivarna planets have been here for many years, officially we are still classed as Earth citizens and following the official statement the other day, the one that directly affects yourself, I realised that in a way it also applied to the whole population of the Nivarna planets. First of all, I mentioned this situation to the members of the Nivarna 7 committee and added that I indeed to voluntarily rescind my citizenship of Earth. Eventually, following approaches being made to the Nivarna 7 community, they all agreed to do the same. Through official and personal approaches, the populations of the other Nivarna planets also agreed to join in. A list is being drawn up that will be forwarded to Earth, while we are still able to contact them."

Javan was astounded.

"It's all thanks to you," Santos said.

"But, I didn't do anything," Javan replied.

"If you hadn't have been here with me, I would never have had the idea in the first place. So thanks to you, we will now be free from Earth and its rules and regulations. We will be a truly independent group of planets, able to make our own decisions. I'd love to see the expression on the face of the official who receives the list of names. From what I've heard of him, the chairman of the NOC will blow a fuse. I wonder how he'll feel when he realises that his job no longer exists!"

The face of the official who received the information was indeed a picture. He was confused by the heading on the document: THE FEDERATION OF NIVARNA PLANETS. He went on to read the contents, which stated that all of the residents of the Nivarna planets were voluntarily removing themselves from the list of Earth citizens. He read it to himself twice, to ensure that he fully grasped the implications: This is going to cause some upset, he said to himself, not daring to say it aloud, just in case anyone was listening.

Normally, a communication of this importance would have been taken to the appropriate person as quickly as possible, rather than sending it through the internal electronic system. The problem was the recipient, the chairman of the NOC. The man had a volatile temper and woe betide the person who brought him bad news.

It was mid-afternoon before the young man knocked on the chairman's office door. He entered the room, handed the chairman the document and exited as quickly as possible. He'd only just managed to close the door behind him, when he heard the roar from within. He almost ran along the corridor but the sound of the chairman's voice didn't seem to decrease in volume.

As the chairman read the document for the fourth time, he came to a decision. "If that's the way they want it to be, so be it. The gloves are off now. Let's see if they're ready to cope with what I have planned for them," he sneered.

CHAPTER 17

LOOKING FOR ANSWERS

As they were preparing to leave the restaurant, they heard something that stopped them in their tracks. An announcement was made on the daily news broadcast from Earth, which was directed to any Earth citizens who were currently visiting, or residing on any of the Nivarna planets, that required them to return to Earth in the next seven days, or their citizenship would be cancelled.

"That's going to put the cat among the pigeons!" said the professor.

"I haven't heard that expression for a long time," replied Dr Stuart.

"Anyway, that announcement certainly messes up our plans." He looked over at Doctor Litarpenko, who nodded in agreement.

"We wanted to work along with you for as long as we deemed necessary. Now we only have a few days before we'll have to board a transport and return home."

"Shall we discuss the implications and have a look at the current information that's been received from the instruments, when we get back to base?" suggested the professor. They left the building and began their journey to the seismology centre.

Hearing the sound of their arrival, Don, one of the two technicians, stepped outside to greet them. "I'm glad that you're back. I was just going to contact you."

"Why?" queried the professor, "has something happened?"

At this juncture the other technician, Pedro, joined in the conversation. "Because of the level of the incoming signals, it has been necessary to alter the sensitivity of the detectors so that they weren't being overloaded. We've had to do this twice so far already today."

"I know that Pedro and I aren't as skilled in deciphering the information from the detectors as you all are, although we know enough to be worried by the information that has been received."

Don stopped abruptly when he realised that their number had increased by two. “I’m sorry for ignoring you – are you two our new members of staff?” he asked.

While the introductions were being made, Professor Lagardé looked at all the information that had been gathered from the probes during the day. Having satisfied himself that he had a good idea of what was taking place, he rejoined the group.

“Is the concern shown by Don and Pedro justified?” Janice asked.

All eyes turned towards the professor. “Come and see the information and judge for yourselves whether we need to be concerned.”

They gathered around the detectors and studied the information that had been collated during the previous thirty-six hours. While scrutinisation of the data took place, the two technicians kept in the background and waited to see if they had been correct. The scientists took their time analysing the material before coming to their individual conclusions, based upon their own specific sphere of interest. When all the conclusions were put together, they agreed that there had been a marked shift in seismic activity, which was increasing in intensity at a far greater rate than had been expected.

The professor turned to the two technicians. “Your concerns were well placed. Well done for spotting the signs of increasing activity. The amount that you’ve had to reduce the sensitivity of the detectors really demonstrates the extreme levels of magma activity that’s taking place inside the planet.”

They moved away to sit at a table and the professor, as team leader, took charge. He suggested that first of all they should hear the information that Dr Litarpenko had obtained for them. “Then we must plan our activities for tomorrow. Sadly, the day after that, our two visitors will have to start their journey back to Earth, so as not to incur the wrath of the authorities. We’ll barely have a chance to get to know you, but the brevity of your time with us isn’t down to you, it’s one of the situations caused by the worsening situation between the Nivarna planets and Earth. Anyway, let’s forget about that for now and see what delights

Ulana has brought us contained within the documents that she 'obtained'."

"Thank you professor," she said. "Both Ian and I are very sorry that our time with you has been cut short. We've really enjoyed meeting you all. You seem to be a very tight-knit team and we feel that you're the best hope that the inhabitants of this planet have. And we hope that if it's possible we'll be able to meet you again sometime in the future."

She then went on to explain what she had uncovered. "I was nearly found out on a few occasions; nosey security guards asking questions about my reason for digging about in the archives. It was obvious that I was the first person in there for many years, as there was a layer of dust on everything and an appreciable amount of cobwebs to be brushed aside before access could be gained to the boxes and filing cabinets. As I don't like spiders you're lucky that I was able to continue and collect all of this information."

"Can I ask something?"

"Of course you can, Don."

"Why is the information on paper? Didn't they use computers back then?"

"Do you mind if I answer that," interjected the professor.

"Of course not. Go ahead," answered Ulana.

"At the time when the Nivarna planets were originally being surveyed, there were some queries as to the security of various electronic systems. Nowadays, the systems we use are far more secure, as they are based on a system of random encryption. Looking back over human history, worries like this have popped up now and again. I remember learning in my history lesson at school of a period in time when some nations' security services actually reverted back to the use of typewriters, as they didn't trust their electronic systems."

Ulana took centre stage once again. "I can see that some of you are puzzled by the word 'typewriter'. Ask the professor later on and he can explain for you, or use your personal computers to look it up. Right – back to the contents of these papers. I'll just summarise it all for now and I'll leave them here when I go, then you can go through them in detail. Quite possibly, there might be some morsel of information that will help you out."

She went on to explain that when the first survey ship landed on the planet, they found some evidence of habitation, although it wasn't planet wide. From the ruins, they established that the previous residents had been a little taller than humans, but there wasn't much else for them to base their summaries on. Some distance away from the ruins there was a large building that was in a much better state of repair. They wanted to examine it closer, but were unable because their radiation alarms operated, so they had to back off. The survey team had a look at the remainder of the planet's surface, but were unable to find any further evidence of any kind of colonisation by whoever had been there in the past. It was obvious that the radioactive building that they found was of some significance to the previous occupiers. Maybe it was part of their preparations for habitation, but then found somewhere more suitable. No one would ever know.

Apart from the radioactive building the planet was deemed suitable for human habitation, following the completion of terra-forming. A specialist team was sent in to deal with the radioactivity and demolish the building where it emanated from, then remove the remains. She went on to explain that there were some drawings detailing the construction of the large radioactive slabs that made up the structure and the mysterious arrangement of pipes that were sunk deep down into the crust and mantle of the planet. It doesn't state where this material was deposited, although it contains details of tests performed on it. The blocks emitted a type of radiation unknown on Earth and the story was similar with the metal of the pipes. Both were alien to Earth's technology.

"So, to sum up," she said, "I surmise that this building that we removed, without understanding its purpose, was some kind of volcanic suppression system way beyond our knowledge and understanding and its removal all those years ago, has slowly developed into the situation you find yourselves in now. I do believe that unless you are able to come up with nothing short of a miracle, this planet will eventually blow itself to pieces."

Silence enveloped the room like a blanket, no one knowing what to say, but each one of them feeling that she was most probably correct. They were frustrated, because they didn't know what to do, or say.

The silence was broken by Chris Fielding. "I appreciate that I'm not the most highly-qualified person here, but to me, Ulana's explanation seems the most logical reason for the problem we are faced with." Everyone nodded in agreement.

His wife, Janice, also entered the discussion at this point. "This is one occasion that I actually agree with Chris and would add that I feel tomorrow would be best spent visiting the farmers that have reported unusual earth movements on their land."

"That's exactly what I was planning," said the professor. "That way we can make the best use of our visiting companions. I have a large amount of administrative work to deal with and the two technicians have readings to take and maintenance schedules to follow. So, if the four of you split yourselves into two teams, I'll provide you with copies of the reports received from the farmers and then you can plan how to make best use of your time."

The three team members left at the seismology centre spent the next day fulfilling their prescribed tasks, but were expectantly waiting for the return of the two teams. They wanted to know what they'd encountered. If the farmers had reported the situations it must be quite serious, as they didn't usually complain about anything. They would deal with a situation themselves. So what they were being presented with was obviously way outside their ability to manage.

As the hours passed by and daylight began to fade, they individually went outside to see if either team could be seen. Eventually, the three of them ended up sitting outside, in the warmth of the early evening, to await the return of the expeditions.

Both of them appeared within a few moments of each other. Professor Lagardé sighed with relief. He had been very worried about the possibility of one of them being involved in some kind of accident. The two transports pulled up outside the centre.

"Hi honey," Chris called out. "I'm home," and as he said it Ulana gave him a playful slap on the shoulder.

"It's obvious that you two have got on well," said the professor. "And how about you, Janice and Ian?" he asked.

"We also got on very well," Janice replied. "It's nice to have someone different to talk to and we've seen some really unusual things."

"I was expecting that you would. Come inside, freshen up and then you can report to us stay-at-homes about all the information you can add to our already large understanding of what's happening on this planet."

They took their seats at the table again to hear what the teams had to say. Apart from the, by now, quite common cracks in the surface and small cones slowly building up, there was a new, dramatic development. On a number of the farms that they visited they discovered that the surface of the fields were changing. Some fields had large bulges, not unlike sand dunes running across them in some cases disappearing into the distance, while others had deep depressions. Overall, this gave the impression that the crust of the planet was undulating, like waves, on top of a sea of magma.

"Did both teams witness this?" the professor asked.

"Yes, we did," they replied.

"I wouldn't mind surmising that if we had the time, we would find that these distortions in the planet's surface are moving all in the same direction and that they will keep reversing with relative flat spots in between the highs and lows," said Ian.

"I agree," said Ulana, "and my supposition made yesterday about the future of the planet, has been made more certain by our findings today. I would suggest that plans to evacuate be drawn up as soon as possible."

"Now we've got all of that out of our systems, let's go and have something to eat and remember, not a word of any of this while we're in the restaurant. It's not possible to say anything in there without someone hearing it," the professor warned them.

"I told you," said Ulana. "You might not have listening

devices under the tables, but you still have to be careful what you say."

"Point taken," the professor replied.

The following morning the staff of the seismology centre met at the space port to say farewell to Ulana and Ian, as they prepared to leave Nivarna 12. There were kisses, shaking of hands and, of course, the professor had the last word. "I would like to thank you both for all the help and information that you've provided. I'll go so far as saying, that we wouldn't have made the progress we have, without your assistance."

Ulana and Ian turned away and just before they passed through planetary control, they both turned around and waved one last time and Janice felt sure that she could see tears on Ulana's cheeks. They were cleared through by the authorities and walked toward the craft that would start their journey back to Earth.

CHAPTER 18

A REVERSAL OF FORTUNE

The three Nivarna delegates were marched along the corridor towards the lift. The people they passed along the way stood flat against the wall, from the moment they saw the security squad, until they had passed by. It appeared that the security staff had a daunting reputation and that people kept well out of their way, if possible.

They all entered the lift and it commenced its journey to the lower levels where the cells were. No one uttered a word, although the minds of the delegates were working overtime, as they tried to come to terms with everything that was taking place and the possible outcomes that could be heading in their direction. No matter how bad they thought their situation was, they couldn't forget they had been assured that whatever transpired they would be safely returned to the Nivarna system.

The lift slowed and then came to a standstill. The doors slid open. On the wall facing them were two signs: to the left the cells and to the right the transport park. They were pushed from behind, in an attempt to get them moving, as they were somewhat reticent. As they left the lift they began to turn left, but much to their surprise they were turned in the opposite direction. The chairman of the Nivarna Operating Committee had ordered the security team to take them to the cells, so why were they heading towards the transport park? This caught them totally off-guard. They wondered whether this was part of the escape plan, or some other unexpected development.

The doors at the end of the corridor led to the outside world and could only be opened by entering a complex collection of letters and numbers onto a keypad. The security team leader had obviously learnt the sequence as he was able to enter it without hesitation. They had only taken a few steps away from the door when they were brought to a halt by a senior officer.

"Who are these men?" he asked the sergeant.

"They're renegades from the Nivarna system, who the Nivarna Operating Committee are sending to Station 34!" he replied.

"Very good," said the officer. "I hope they get everything they deserve."

The delegates couldn't believe what they had just heard. The leader of the security squad had just lied to a superior officer, but there was something else. There was a familiarity in the tone of his voice and the way that he spoke. They just couldn't put their finger on it. They looked at one another, as they tried to fathom out what was taking place. They didn't dare to speak out as they didn't know what the consequences would be, but they were worried about their eventual destination. What was Station 34? And what would happen to them when they arrived, that's if Station 34 was to actually be their destination?

Twilight was descending as they were marched across the transport park, finally coming to a halt beside a prisoner transport vehicle. The delegates were placed in the rear of the van, then the doors were shut and locked behind them. The security squad climbed into the front half of the van. The delegates were separated from the security squad by a barrier that comprised two sections: the bottom half was a plain metal panel, the top half was mesh that they could see through and also hear what the security squad were saying.

The driver switched on the power and the two lights on the roof began to rotate, casting long red beams across the surrounding area. No one said a word as the vehicle began to move forward, manoeuvring its way through the other parked vehicles. Slowly, but carefully, it was steered towards the main gate. When it arrived, other security guards emerged from a small building to check the van's paperwork, along with the transportation paperwork for its passengers. The delegates watched from the rear of the van, waiting to see what was going to happen. They were surprised when the paperwork was accepted and the van was waved through.

They were unable to work out what was taking place, but they realised that there had been a great deal of planning and preparation involved. Maybe this was the rescue plan. If not, what was going on?

Driving out of the security headquarters onto the road network wasn't a problem. The moment drivers saw the red lights on the roof they immediately stopped to allow the security vehicle priority. A similar situation occurred on the roads. All kinds of vehicles pulled over to the side to allow the security van to pass by, then continued their journey afterwards. With the roads effectively clear, it didn't take long before they reached the outskirts of the city. As they passed the city boundary, something happened that stunned the delegates. They'd been surprised on a number of occasions during the whole episode, but nothing like this had happened before.

The sergeant, who was sitting beside the driver, turned to him and said in a broad Nivarnan accent, "I didn't think we were going to get away with that!"

"It was a bit hairy at times, wasn't it," the driver replied.

The delegates looked at one another , not believing what they were hearing. Noticing what was happening in the back of the van, the security officer closest to them spoke through the grille.

"I'm sorry that we had to lock you in, but it had to look authentic. We're all from various Nivarna planets and were paced here on Earth just in case we were needed and, as it turned out, we were."

* * *

The chairman of the Nivarna Operating Committee wasn't having a good day. He'd spent a large part of the morning in a confrontational meeting with the Nivarna Supply Committee, centring on the chief supply officer. Then he didn't like the food that was on offer at the canteen at lunchtime. Even the afternoon didn't improve, because the delegates from the Nivarna were presented to the NOC. By this time his rage had been slowly building up. Then came the cherry on the cake.

He was summoned to the commissioner's office that was situated on the top floor of the building. The chairman was always fascinated by the way the commissioner knew exactly what was taking place in all of the departments that were based in the building. So he wasn't particularly surprised when the commissioner was fully conversant with the meeting with the Nivarna delegates that afternoon. The culmination of the meeting was that the NOC was to be wound up at the end of the month, as it wasn't needed now that the Nivarna planets had effectively declared independence. Then came the chairman's biggest blow. As they were closing down the NOC, his services would no longer be needed. In other words, they were making him redundant. He was thanked for all that he had done and was immediately ushered out of the office.

He was in a daze, as he made his way back to his office. Closing down the NOC had been a distinct possibility following the development from the Nivarna planets, but he thought that he might be transferred to another department. Being made redundant wasn't something that he had considered. By now, he was close to boiling point. He'd been angry before, now he was at the point where he was ready to erupt and, like a volcano, cause massive destruction. He needed a safety valve and decided to let rip at the delegates that had been sent to the cells.

The custody officer picked up his communicator and winced slightly when he saw the identity of the caller. What does he want, he thought. As it was likely to be a rather loud call, he switched it to speakers so that he could have the unit on his desk, which was better than having it clamped to his ear. He depressed the receive button and then sat back in his chair.

"Hello. This is the chairman of the NOC."

"Good afternoon, chairman, how can I help you?" the officer replied.

"Is it all right for me to visit the three men that I sent down to the cells about two hours ago?"

There was a pause, then the officer replied. "I haven't had any new prisoners today. In fact, I only have two cells occupied at the moment."

There was a further pause, but while this one took place the officer could almost hear the chairman coming to the boil.

"What do you mean?" the chairman shouted. "I sent three men down to the cells and they were accompanied by a security squad. That's eight men. They couldn't just disappear, could they? Explain that to me."

"Leave it with me and I'll ask around, in case anyone else saw anything," the custody officer replied, feeling much relieved when he ended the conversation. He left his office, looking for anybody that could explain why these prisoners had gone missing. He did eventually find one person that had seen a security squad with some men, but they went out to the transport park.

The custody officer contacted the NOC chairman to relay this information to him, information that wasn't received very well. To say that the man was angry would be an understatement. The officer had never known him get this bad before. He knew the chairman had a vile temper, but never as nasty as it was when he received this information. He could have sworn that he heard the chairman sobbing, just before the conversation was terminated.

The chairman was a broken man. The prisoners having escaped was the last straw. His already high blood pressure rocketed and the demand on his heart became more than it could bear. Years of ignoring medical advice had finally caught up with him and his heart gave out – it ceased beating. He fell off his chair and hit his head on the corner of his desk as he slumped to the floor. He wasn't a small man and made an appreciable amount of noise when he hit the floor, taking his chair down with him. He lay there, a bloodied gash to his forehead, the chair across his legs, his days of anger brought to an abrupt end.

His collapse had made such a noise that it was heard in the adjacent office. The occupants volunteered the bravest amongst them to see what had happened. The reluctant man meekly tapped on the chairman's door, expecting the usual tirade of abuse, but nothing happened – silence. He cautiously opened the door and looked inside. When he saw the chairman sprawled out his first-aid training took over. He placed his fingers on the chairman's neck, but was unable to find a pulse. He used the communication system on the desk to call for medical assistance, relating to them the nature of the emergency along with the room number where the victim lay.

The medical team arrived a few moments later, having used an override that caused the lift to travel faster than normal. They attached the 'paddles' of a defibrillator to the chairman's chest, switched the unit on and stood back. After a few seconds the machine said, "No pulse" and then administered a shock. This happened four times with a higher level of shock delivered each time. Finally, the machine stated that there was a weak pulse, but they didn't disconnect the unit in case the heart stopped again. The medics placed a blanket over the chairman and a pillow under his head to make him as comfortable as possible, given that he most likely wasn't aware of what was taking place.

When the team from the hospital arrived they congratulated the building's in-house medics for bringing the patient – for that's what he was now – back from the point of death. They had brought an anti-grav stretcher with them and struggled slightly to place the patient upon it.

"He's a big lad, isn't he?" one of the team stated.

"Was he a gentle giant, or the opposite?" his companions asked.

The volunteer, whose colleagues were now watching from the door, informed them that he had a somewhat fearsome reputation.

"The nurses won't put up with any of that kind of behaviour," the third and senior member of the team stated. "I'd just like to record the details of the incident," he said to the volunteer, "while they take him down to the ambulance, if you wouldn't mind."

The chairman's reign of terror was over.

Meanwhile, the custody officer had been trying to track down the missing prisoners. He had established that they were from the Nivarna system by talking to a couple of members of the NOC board. They both confirmed that they had been sent to the cells and were accompanied by a security detail.

Back in his office, he poured himself a drink and thought about the situation while he sipped the hot liquid. Then it suddenly came to him. They'd want to get off the planet as quickly as possible and the only place they could do that was the space port. He grabbed his communicator and contacted the officers at the space port's side gate, that was exclusively used by the security department.

He revealed who he was and fortunately the officer he was speaking to knew him, so that made things easier. He explained the situation and the officer confirmed that a group matching the description had entered the area a few moments earlier.

"They'll try to board a craft and get off of the planet!" the custody officer yelled. He heard the officer shouting orders and then a vehicle start up. They used small four-seaters that were very manoeuvrable around the parked craft – and then the communicator went dead.

The space port floodlights came on and were followed by the sounding of a siren.

"They're onto us," said the sergeant. "Don't worry, we haven't far to go."

They rounded a large cargo transport that had the name of the merchant printed on the side. Under different circumstances they might have paid a little more attention to it, as it was somewhat different from the transport that they were used to. They passed by a small company passenger carrier and took a sharp left turn and approached an anti-grav passenger transport that was designed to carry people to larger orbital craft that weren't allowed to land on the surface. The vehicle stopped.

"That's as close as we can go," the sergeant stated. "We'll have to make a run for it now."

The three delegates didn't understand why this was, although it was explained later, but they ran as if their lives depended on it, which they did, as the security vehicles had almost caught up with them.

The delegates didn't realise that the pursuing pack were shooting at them, as the weapons they used were silent. But the projectiles they fired were deadly. That particular kind of projectile had been banned throughout the world, although they were occasionally used by the security services, this being one of the occasions that they were employed.

They were approximately forty feet from their destination when one of their team was hit. He staggered on for a few steps and then fell face down onto the ground.

"Keep running," shouted the sergeant. "There's nothing we can do for him!"

The remainder of the squad made it to the passenger craft, the doors slammed behind them and even before they had time to settle, it rose off the ground and shot off up into the air, while the space port security staff vainly tried to shoot it down.

The sergeant could sense a change in attitude from the delegates, which was most apparent when he spoke directly to them. To sort this problem out he asked them what was wrong.

"We think that you acted callously when one of your associates was gunned down," one of the delegates stated.

"Callousness didn't enter into any decision," replied the sergeant, "because of the type of projectiles that they were using. It's similar to an old-style bullet, although the tip contains a deadly poison that was synthesised from a combination of poisons obtained from the Amazonian Indians that lived in an area which, at one time, was called the Amazonian Rain Forest. That's before it was devastated. Anyway, when Jamie, that was his name by the way, was hit, he was dead from that moment on and there wasn't anything that anyone could have done for him."

"Thank you for explaining," another of the delegates said. "Maybe you can tell us why we had to leave our vehicles and run the last few feet, while you're at it."

"By all means," the Sergeant said. "The vehicle we're currently travelling in is powered by an anti-gravity drive, the same type that we use on the Nivarna planets."

It seemed surreal to see a 'sergeant of the security service' speak about the Nivarna system, although they slowly began to get used to it. He began to realise it for himself and explained to the delegates that they had the choice of having them in their uniforms or in their underwear. The unanimous decision was in favour of the uniforms.

"However," the sergeant said, "let's return to the reason for our mad dash for our current craft. Under usual circumstances all vehicles are removed from the area, before the anti-grav drive is powered up, because of the effect on the metal contained within the construction of the vehicle. We didn't have that option. The craft had to be ready to go, at a moment's notice. Therefore we had to run the final few feet as it wasn't safe to get any closer to the craft."

Everything returned to normal following these explanations, spending the remainder of the journey to their interplanetary transport swapping names, comparing Nivarna planets and personal information.

"There she is!" exclaimed the pilot. All of the passengers walked to the front of the craft to look out of the observation windows. Caught in the beams from the craft's headlights was the unmistakable shape of a transport craft. Normally such a craft would have a surface of polished lightweight alloy, although this particular one was totally black. Another notable variation was the lack of an identification number. After seeing this unusual craft, they all had questions to ask the crew on board. They also wondered what other secrets were located within that matt-black hull.

The passenger craft latched onto the docking unit of the transport, allowing them to leave one craft and enter the other. The pilot was the last to leave as he had to set the autopilot system of the passenger transport, so that the craft remained in orbit, ready to be retrieved by Earth.

"After all, we don't want to be accused of stealing their craft, do we?" the pilot said.

"If that's the case, aren't they going to miss a transport craft?"

the sergeant asked.

"Let's all get settled and on our way before we spent time answering questions," said one of the crew members. They all congregated in the eating area, while the crew persuaded the great mass of metal to begin moving. The transport build-up speed incredibly quickly, even the passengers felt the speed increasing. They all had undertaken journeys in transports before, but this encounter was different from anything they'd previously experienced.

Once the transport craft was at cruising speed, the computer was engaged to direct the ship back along the well-worn path to Nivarna 1. Before leaving the flight deck the pilot performed a quick diagnostic on the alarm systems, then he was happy to leave the ship under the control of the automatic systems and he could take a break.

Joining the rest of the ship's company, he poured himself a large coffee into a mug with 'The Boss' painted on the side.

"Drink up," he said, "this is premium Earth coffee." His encouragement wasn't wasted, as the remainder of the coffee drinkers grabbed mugs and filled them to the brim.

"I didn't hear if any of the Nivarna planets would be suitable but I purloined some coffee plants and tea bushes, so that the residents of the Nivarna system can enjoy some quality beverages," said a crew member, "and they're safety tucked away in a couple of the holds, which have been adjusted to the correct temperatures and humidity."

Once everyone started to relax, the questions began to flow.

"Won't we be accused of stealing this transport?"

"No," was the answer to that one, "because the craft doesn't exist. Well, not so far as the records go. It was built over an appreciable time from spare parts. When we ordered spares, we always ordered more than we needed for work on the fleet. Eventually we had gathered enough parts to build this craft. When complete, it was parked in geo-synchronous orbit over the South Pole of Earth, as there was minimal traffic in that area." They were congratulated on such a devious scheme.

"Won't vehicles from Earth be able to catch us?"

"No way. Our engineer – take a bow James – has a marvellous touch when it comes to engines, having adjusted the standard engine that's normally fitted to these transports to produce fifty per cent more power, which you may have felt when we got underway. I don't know how he manages it, although I'm glad he can. Also, just in case you're wondering, the craft is painted in a special matt black paint, that renders us invisible to visual and electronic tracking systems."

While all this was being revealed, the craft was getting closer and closer to the Nivarna system, returning all of them to their families and compatriots.

CHAPTER 19

ALL ABOARD FOR THE SKYLARK

For many months, while the potential crew members were being gathered together for their courses and orientation, Explorer 1 was being constructed in a geo-synchronous orbit above the space port that they would eventually leave from. Such an orbit made sense, as it allowed the pre-fabricated parts to be carried up to the construction site in the shortest distance possible. Because of the size of some of the parts, extra large anti-grav aircraft had to be constructed while, on a smaller scale, special versions of the standard anti-grav crafts were built that were twice the size of the normal passenger craft, which were used for carrying individual items, such as catering equipment, up to the site. When the construction phase was completed, these smaller craft would be fitted out with seating and used to transport crew members up to Explorer 1.

The day had finally arrived when the first crew members would leave Earth's surface and travel up to the newly-fitted Explorer 1. Those who had specific functions were the first on board: crew members such as the caterers, flight crew, medical staff, along with the military, who had been re-designated security staff for this voyage. These crew members needed to familiarise themselves with the layout of the ship and their specific areas of responsibility. As more and more of the crew came aboard, Explorer 1 slowly came alive, becoming a glowing city in the sky that could clearly be seen from Earth.

When the full complement of crew had been on board for just over a week, almost everything had been checked out and any faults found had been rectified. There was only one part of the ship that had yet to be tested to its full capacity and that was the experimental engine. The crew had tested out the equipment on the flight deck, including some of the minor engine circuits. All the computer simulations that they were able to run had been successfully completed. The final task to be undertaken before blast off, was to load a variety of ancillary items into the hold.

This included two standard and two double-size anti-grav craft, now fitted out with new seating. It was planned for these craft to be used to carry crew members down to the surface of Nivarna 12.

The maiden voyage of Explorer 1 was imminent. The planned destination was Nivarna 12, as that was to be the extent of its range. Well, that's what they had been told, but the military had other ideas, which was why there hadn't been any problems, or delays, in obtaining funds for the project. Even though the destination was the Nivarna system, the department overseeing the Explorer project hadn't been informed that the relationship between Earth and the Nivarna planets had become somewhat acrimonious. Keeping the Independence Declaration under wraps, had been one of the final decisions made by the now defunct Nivarna Operating Committee, fearing unrest by the population when they realised the implications. The last thing the authorities wanted was for the general population to begin to panic and then start to demonstrate or even riot. So they decided to keep quiet and deal with any problems as they arose.

As the days passed by all the minor faults and problems were rectified, until Explorer 1 was passed as being fit for the planned flight. By the time this occurred, Stephen had become used to being out of the khaki uniform that he had worn ever since he had signed up for the military. He now wore the less formal relaxed style of clothing that was standard onboard the ship. To identify members of the security staff their jumpers bore epaulettes of crimson, whereas Stephen's were purple denoting his senior rank.

Doug was by now used to being called 'Doc' everywhere he went and secretly rather enjoyed being recognised by everyone. The equipment provided for the medical department was the most up to date possible, which was in marked contrast with the somewhat sparse set-up at the base where he had been previously assigned. He had already performed a couple of minor operations and had found the whole installation a joy to use. The nursing staff that worked along with him were pleasant, knowledgeable and highly competent, which made Doug's job far more enjoyable and a great deal easier and he was grateful for the efforts put forward by the nursing staff section.

As for Chris, everyone on board had become used to seeing him hobbling around and watched him steadily improve as his bones knitted themselves back together again. At one time he felt sure that his prospective space trip was over when he broke his ankle. He was so thankful that Doug had been able to persuade the board in charge of the project, to allow him on the journey as part of an official medical experiment. Chris would be the first person to have a documented record made of how a fracture would heal in a space environment.

From the time that Explorer 1 had become visible from Earth, there had been a great deal of interest in the whole project shown by members of the public. So it was agreed, by all the parties concerned, to allow a TV crew on board the ship. This crew was made up of volunteers, who would travel up to Explorer 1, spending some time examining the ship and getting to know the crew members, interviewing them about themselves along with their role on board the ship. They would remain on board during the initial journey, so that a record was made of the first large-scale use of the experimental engine and then, if it was successful, the return journey back to Earth.

As Explorer 1 was a military project there had to be a formal inspection visit by a high-ranking officer, when he would be shown around the ship by the pilot, who was formally in charge. At this point they didn't know who the officer would be, although they had been told that the visit would take place two days before the official blast off. The next few days were spent cleaning, tidying cupboards, bunks etc; all the bits and pieces that a formal military inspection would require.

The identity of the visiting officer finally came through. It was to be Field-Marshal Sir Timothy Franks. The use of such archaic terms as Sir and Lord weren't normally used in these modern times, although some of the long-established families insisted on hanging onto the terminology. As most people didn't pay much attention to such terms, it was easier to let things be as they were, ensuring that no one on either side became upset.

They were informed that the visit would take place in two days time, so it was easy to ascertain that blast off was scheduled for midday, four days hence. The following day was spent preparing the crew for the formal presentation to the visiting officer. For the first time they would be wearing their dress uniform, which consisted of a light-blue coverall, that was worn over the white everyday uniform. For the majority of the crew, wearing the coverall was the first opportunity they had to see the large circular 'mission badge' which was mounted on the right breast pocket and was copied from the badges of the very first space flight missions, way back in the 1960s.

The day of the inspection arrived and exactly on time and the anti-grav vehicle docked with Explorer 1, allowing the visiting officer, along with his entourage, to commence their inspection. They were shown around all the usual areas, questions were answered and requests to deviate from the formal inspection protocol were honoured. Then came the speech to the crew. It was, no doubt, one that had been presented in similar situations many times before and, to be quite honest, the majority of the crew paid little attention to it. They were on parade because they had to be.

Finally came the formal dinner. In attendance were the visitors, along with all the department heads. It was pleasant enough and the visiting officer did his best to lighten the atmosphere with a few well-practiced anecdotes, which caused a measured amount of laughter. All the participants made the best of a difficult situation and it's fair to say that the visitors were as relieved to be on the journey home as the crew of Explorer 1 were to see them leave.

With the visit over and done with, they could concentrate on preparing for the blast off. The flight crew ran and re-ran the navigation and life support test simulations, until they were sick and tired of watching them. The department heads went through what was expected to happen when the new engine kicked in. As far as the simulations that had been run by the medics, who were associated with the engine design department, they indicated that the crew would become unconscious during the time the engine was running, due to the effect of the distortion drive.

The day before blast off found the ship rife with speculation about what would take place when the drive fired up. No one really knew, the unknown being the main attraction for a large number of crew members. Would they survive? Would Explorer 1 explode? No one had a definitive answer. It was, therefore, a rather apprehensive crew that retired to bed that night, knowing that all their questions would be answered within the next twenty-three hours, that's if they were still alive.

The atrium was a multipurpose space, which was used as a dining hall, meeting room and could also be rearranged for use as a cinema. Now the cinema seats were set out, with the addition of a seat belt on each one. The belt was for use during the inaugural flight of Explorer 1, which included the first full-scale test of the new engine.

Even though blast off wasn't due to happen until midday, crew members began to gather in the atrium, once the breakfast servings had concluded and everything was cleaned up and packed away. By 11.30 almost all of the crew had arrived, chosen their seat and snapped their seatbelts closed. There are always a few late arrivals and this time was no different. The department heads moved along the rows of seats, checking the seatbelts to ensure that they were securely locked. It wasn't really known whether they were needed or not, although it had been decided to fit them as a precaution.

At five minutes to lift off, all of the crew were seated and securely strapped in place. For the first time the flight crew appeared on the huge viewing screen on the end wall of the atrium. A countdown clock also appeared on the screen. When it reached thirty seconds to go, the atrium became unusually silent and all the chatter died away. The final countdown commenced. Crew members clutched the hands of whoever was sitting next to them.

At Zero, the pilot pressed a large square button on the control panel and the solid fuel jet engine burst into life. Explorer 1 began to move. It wouldn't be until the ship was approximately a third of the way to Mars before the new engine would be utilised. This had been decided upon, as the scientists were unsure of the effect that the distortion drive could have had on Earth's orbit. So conventional rockets were used to move Explorer 1 well away from Earth before the new engine was engaged.

The population of Earth weren't the only ones interested in Explorer 1 and its new engine. Outside the range of Earth's scanners was an alien ship, a smaller version of the craft that had destroyed Transport 113. It had been placed there since the construction of Explorer 1 had commenced. From the amount of knowledge they had gathered about the whole project including the 'secret' engine, they obviously had a comprehensive network of information gatherers on Earth, the aliens having a greater amount of knowledge on the project than most people on Earth.

As Explorer 1 slowly gathered momentum, the alien craft maintained its distance by running a parallel course. Eventually the solid fuel rockets had burnt all of their fuel and ceased to function. Explorer 1 continued its forward motion, which by space craft standards was rather slow. They were now far enough away from Earth to engage the engine. They had reached the point of no return. The countdown clock reappeared on the screen, starting at the one minute mark. The engine had been through its warm-up phase while the rockets were burning. The pilot lifted the cover from over the 'Engine Engage' button, as it was still preferred that a human performed the function rather than leaving the operation to a computer.

The engine began to create its operational field and crew members began to feel themselves drifting into unconsciousness. As this happened the alien craft emitted a narrow beam electro-magnetic pulse (EMP) towards the flight deck of Explorer 1. The intent was to corrupt all the electronic equipment, such as the navigational and engine control circuits, leaving the ship to run without control or direction.

As the pilot began to slide into unconsciousness he saw all the displays on his control panel disappear at the same time. He was unable to do anything. He saw his two compatriots reflected in the now blank display panel and hoped to attract their attention. It was too late, they had already been affected by the ever-increasing engine field.

No one on Earth had any knowledge of what had taken place. They were all waiting to see what happened when the engine reached full power and the drive kicked in. A small unmanned craft had followed Explorer 1 to its current position, the onboard cameras providing live pictures to the world-wide audience.

The commentator was providing a countdown to the expected point when the drive would engage. She was spot-on: three – two – one – zero. On zero, Explorer 1 seemed to disappear, as the ship was transported out of normal space, into the distorted continuum that the engine created. It had started a journey not to Nivarna 12 as planned, because the navigational array wasn't functioning. As far as Earth was concerned, Explorer 1 would never be heard from again.

The alien craft switched off the EMP beam and began its journey to the location of their next mission. There wasn't any possible way they were able to track the Earth ship as it wasn't travelling in normal space. So long as their sabotage had been successful their superiors would be happy. They had determined the military's real reason for developing such a craft, which was to be able to track down the location of the alien's home planet. That was something that the aliens didn't want to happen – at any cost.

CHAPTER 20

HARVEST

Following the Independence Declaration, there were a number of reassignments within the Nivarna group of planets. Many farmers began to grow fruit which was for their own use and were unable to produce enough to supply the whole system. As fruit was necessary for the health of all of the Nivarna citizens, Nivarna 10 was designated as a fruit growing planet. There were a number of reasons for this choice. First, the soil on Nivarna 10 was extremely fertile with all of the required minerals to ensure good crops and secondly, regardless of the weather control systems, the planet's sun provided radiation that would encourage the plants and trees to grow plentifully. All the weather control system did was to keep the temperature constant over the planet's surface.

A search was made for any farmer that had experience of fruit growing and they were asked to move to Nivarna 10. The same system that was used to move farmers around so that Nivarna 11 could become the livestock planet was employed. There was a shuffling around of farmers and their families, so that fruit production farmers all ended up on Nivarna 10 and those who were displaced were spread throughout the Nivarna system.

Nirvana 1 had, by default, become the planet where decisions were made, effectively the ruling planet, although it was never actually labelled as such. It was suggested that it would be conducive if the calendars of all of the planets could be unified, so everyone was at least on the same day of the week. The problem was that all of the planets had differing rotational durations. So the day length varied from planet to planet, which would make it difficult for all the planets to be able to be on the same day of the week as they'd soon slip out of synchronisation. A number of chronologists were assigned to the task, but as yet they'd been unable to come up with a universally acceptable solution.

It was Wednesday morning on Nivarna 10 and the farmers were interested in comparing the growth of their crops with their fellow farmers. Preeta walked up the track that led back to the farmhouse, having completed the morning inspection of her vines. She was astounded by the growth of the grapes, which was due to the modified plant that had been developed on Earth, as part of the early attempts to produce the amount of food required. Although the horticulturists were very successful, there just wasn't enough untainted land available on Earth to produce the amount of food needed. It was at that time the idea of the Nivarna planets was first mooted.

Preeta walked into her kitchen and sat down. She was quite puffed out from walking up and down the rows of vines. "I'm just not used to this terrain," she said out loud. She was most likely correct, although she didn't take her advancing years into account.

Preeta was an enigma. People had tried to find out about her, but she wasn't very forthcoming and her official records were minimal. They had learnt that she had been widowed many years earlier, although the exact date when this occurred, coupled with any information concerning her husband, seemed to be a closely guarded secret. There had been a number of suitors over the years, but despite their best attempts nothing ever came of their advances. Preeta seemed to be happy on her own, living her life the way she wanted.

She sat by the kitchen table, lost in her thoughts, when her communicator burst into life. It took her a few moments to return to reality and respond to the communicator's incessant call. It was her one and only male friend, Jason, who had been her neighbour on Nirvana 4 where they had been arable farmers.

"Morning matey," Jason said, "how are you today? How are the vines doing? You should see the size of the apples, lemons and apricots on my trees!"

"All right, bighead," Preeta replied, "my grapes are doing really well. It takes me back to my days on Earth, when I worked at a French chateau, tending the vines. The highlight of the year was always the grape harvest." Jason could almost hear her tears as she continued. "That's until the toxins in the rain and the overall levels of pollution got too much for the plants and they were unable to grow properly anymore."

Jason knew that he had to try and lift her mood, so he manoeuvred the conversation back to her vines. "How long before your first harvest here on Nivarna 10?" he asked.

Thinking about her own grape harvest seemed to be the stimulus required. "I'm not too sure. I'm not used to the rate of growth that these vines seem able to sustain, although I don't think it will be very long now."

"I look forward to joining you on that happy day," Jason said.

Preeta felt better now. She'd enjoyed thinking back to her days in France. I wonder if Jason picked up that I used to speak French, she thought. I wonder if I revealed too much? I don't like people knowing too much about me. They can speculate as much as they like, but my private history is mine and that's the way I want to keep it. I can't sit here all day, I've got work to do and a harvest to prepare for.

The communicator was left on the kitchen table, set to take a message from anyone who called. She didn't like taking it with her as she found it too distracting.

When Jason retired to bed that night his head was so full of thoughts about the impending harvest, that it took him some time to fall asleep. He was restless during the night and began to shiver. Eventually, his discomfort woke him up. He was really cold, so he put on a heavy jumper and then another duvet over the bed, hoping that these additions would warm him up a little. As he waited for sleep to make a welcome return, he speculated that he must be unwell, maybe he'd caught a cold off someone, or maybe he had a chill. He finally fell asleep with these thoughts going round his mind.

He awoke early the following morning, having spent the night in a fitful sleep. When he opened the bedroom curtains, the reason for the chill in the air and his disturbed night's sleep became apparent. The window panes were covered in frost. It was no wonder that the room felt cold. He pulled the sleeve of his jumper down over his hand and used it to remove a circle of frost. He peered through the peephole that he'd created and was astounded to see a covering of frost wherever he looked. How is this happening, he thought, the climate control system must have gone crazy?

Jason was mesmerised by the view, until his brain reminded him of the effect that a frost like this would have on his crops. He was deep in thought when his bedside communicator suddenly activated. He walked over to the bed and responded to the call. It was his friend and fellow orchard grower, Carlos, who lived just a few farms away.

"Do you realise what the time is?" was Jason's greeting. (It was just after 5am.)

"Never mind what time it is, have you looked outside this morning?"

"Yes, I have," Jason replied, "and I couldn't believe what I saw. How bad is it in your neck of the woods?"

"Well, it's most likely as bad as it is where you are. I've spoken to a number of farmers over here and it seems to be the same all over. What's Preeta think about it?"

"It's strange that I haven't heard from her. I'll get sorted out and if I can't raise her, I'll go over there and see what's happening."

"Keep me up to date with what's going on, will you?"

"The moment that I find something out, I'll let you know. See ya later," Jason answered.

"Cheers," Carlos replied and the communicator switched off.

* * *

Jason's transport pod came to a halt outside the front of Preeta's farmhouse. He disembarked and shivered in the chill air that surrounded him. He did not hesitate for long in the coldness and followed the footpath that ran around the side of the building and clearly led him to the back door. He knocked and knocked again. Not receiving a response, he slowly opened the door and looked inside. As expected, there was Preeta's communicator on the kitchen table. She was obviously out among her beloved vines, examining the damage that had been done to the newly-developed grapes. Jason mentally prepared himself for a walk in the cold, not being used to such temperatures any more. He was accustomed to the temperate conditions that were ideal for growing fruits that the weather control system was supposed to maintain. Clearly something had gone wrong, causing this dramatic drop in temperature that had destroyed the emerging crops on this part of Nivarna 10.

Even though it was now mid-morning, there was still a heavy covering of frost on the ground, that displayed Preeta's footprints enabling Jason to track her down. It didn't take as long as he expected. The air was cold and heavy, every small sound breaking the silence that hung over the land. Jason shivered and pulled his coat tighter around him. As he adjusted the coat he heard a noise. It was the sound of crying, then he knew that Preeta couldn't be far away, even though he'd never known her to cry before.

Jason walked past the end of two more rows of vines, taking a look along the long rows of plants each time. As he passed the end of another row he saw her. She was about halfway along the row, sitting on the cold soil, with her head in her hands. He walked down the incline towards her and even though she must have heard his shoes crunching on the frost, she never reacted.

As he arrived alongside her, he never uttered a word but sat down beside her. Jason reached out to put his arm around her and then hesitated. He was unsure whether it was the right thing to do. Although he'd known Preeta for many years, there hadn't been any physical contact between them. She'd never even invited Jason to her farmhouse. He pondered for what seemed like hours, but was actually only a couple of minutes. Jason made his decision. It was now or never. He wouldn't be presented with an opportunity like this again.

He put his arm around her shoulders and was thrilled when she snuggled into him. All she said was, "My grapes, my grapes – look at them – they're ruined."

The two of them sat there for ages, until Jason's bottom was becoming uncomfortably cold and he couldn't stand it any longer. “Once this problem is sorted out, we’ll all be able to grow a new crop and all this will become an unpleasant memory. Come on, let’s go up to the house and I’ll make you a hot drink and we can both warm ourselves up.” Preeta responded like a meek lamb, taking the hand he proffered to help her up onto her feet. With their arms around each other, they walked up the footpath back to the farmhouse.

This deviant weather pattern occurred only in the area that was approaching its first harvest; in fact, the first harvest on Nivarna 10. The planet was split up into growing areas so that a constant supply of fruit could be supplied to the whole Nivarna system, all year round. (The term ‘year’ is a little subjective, as all of the Nivarna planets take different amounts of time to complete their solar orbit. The longest solar orbit, or year, was Nivarna 2, so that was chosen to be the standard Nivarna year.) No one noticed that the weather control system had only failed in one specific area. This wasn’t surprising, as they were more concerned with fixing the system, so that the growth pattern could be re-instigated and the damaged crops re-grown.

As the Nivarna system was being set up in the first place, the now defunct Nivarna Operating Committee ensured that each planet was well supplied with technicians who were able to repair and maintain the variety of electronic and mechanical equipment that was in daily use. There was one area where this rule did not apply. That was the care of the weather control satellites. Such was the NOC’s trust in the resilience of the system that a lone technician had that responsibly, although as the Nivarna system had grown, he’d had the sense to realise that as he grew older he wouldn’t be able to fulfil his remit any longer. His plan was to have a technician on each planet, who was able to deal with any problems that arose with the system.

While the Nivarna system was still able to order items from Earth, he gathered together enough parts to provide each planet with a full maintenance kit in case of any problems. He realised that trying to order specialised anti-grav vehicles was pushing it a little too far. As each of the Nivarna planets used anti-grav vehicles, he modified one on each planet, so that it was able to travel up to the orbit of the satellites. This involved fitting booster rockets, along with their appropriate control systems. The rockets would lift the craft high enough to allow 'hands-on' maintenance, if the satellites couldn't be re-booted from the planet's surface.

By mid-morning, Bernie McBaine had attempted to contact the satellite from the surface of Nivarna 10, using the specialised equipment designed to re-set the satellite into a test mode and uncover any specific problems. But it wasn't having any of that and refused to respond to the instructions being sent to it. After his third attempt to contact the rogue satellite, there was only one course of action left.

The modified anti-grav craft was soon on scene and Bernie loaded all the appropriate equipment, spare parts and the two space suits required to facilitate hands-on maintenance. The air tanks for the suits were checked over as were the spare tanks, just in case they were required. His companion on this maintenance run was a tall girl of African descent, called Liesa Wadham. This would be her first spacewalk and was necessary for her to experience as part of her training as a weather control system technician.

Just over two hours later the anti-grav vehicle landed, mission complete. When asked what had happened, Bernie replied, "I'm not too sure at the moment, but there had been a catastrophic failure in the control systems. In all my years, I've never seen that level of failure before. When I've analysed the faulty circuits on the bench, I'll be able to build up a more complete picture of what happened and whether there's anything that can be done to prevent it happening again."

"How did you manage with your first spacewalk, Leisa?"

"It was amazing," she replied. "I've never experienced anything like it before and can't wait to do it again."

"The only problem is," Bernie interjected, "is that there has to be another failure of the system. But there's the training course for those who haven't done anything like it before."

"Is the system up and running now?"

"Yes," replied Bernie, "but it will take a few hours before the system locks in with the other satellites and then it will begin to have an effect on this part of the planet."

* * *

Unseen by human eyes, the alien craft that had used its EMP beam to cause the devastating damage to the Earth ship, Explorer 1, had used the same beam to damage the weather control satellite at Nivarna 10. Their remit was to disrupt human schemes and cause problems, hoping to discourage them in their plans. The alien's two missions having been completed, it was time for them to return to their home planet and leave the monitoring of the humans to other craft. It appeared that their plan was slowly making progress and appreciated that it would take a long time to come to fruition. But with their extended lifespan, it didn't really matter how long it took.

* * *

When Jason woke the next morning he was hot, so hot that he was sweating. All of the bedcovers that he'd been using during the previous cold nights were on the floor, scattered around the bed. It didn't take him long to realise that the weather control system was slowly adjusting itself, following the repairs that had been made. He opened the bedroom curtains and was presented with a verdant green, that had replaced the while frostiness that he'd become accustomed to.

He hadn't been so keen to get the day started since the frost had arrived. As he ate his breakfast, the communicator began to receive a number of communications from inquisitive farmers, enquiring about conditions in his neighbourhood. Although he appreciated all those calls, there was only one call he was hoping for. As he sipped his coffee he thought: Maybe it's up to me to call her? So he selected Preeta's details and waited. He heard it make the connection and start to buzz. For a moment he thought that she wasn't going to answer, but when she did he couldn't think of anything to say.

"Hello Jason," she said. "How are you this lovely morning?" The moment he heard her voice it enabled him to speak again and the conversation got underway. They talked and talked. It wasn't until he looked at the clock on the wall that he realised how long they'd been chatting. Preeta obviously realised the same thing and said, "That's the best conversation I've had with anyone for years, but I think we'd better go and get some work done! By the way, how would you like to come round for dinner after work tonight?"

Jason was stunned. What he'd most desired for years was now going to take place. He was brought back to reality by Preeta's voice on the communicator.

"Are you still there, Jason?"

"Oh, yes I am! And I'd be delighted to accept your kind offer!"

"That's good. Don't expect anything too fancy, I'll do what I can."

"That would be marvellous," Jason replied. "I'll await your call and come and give you a hand getting everything ready. Would that be all right?

"Lovely," Preeta replied. "See you this evening. Bye for now."

The communicator indicated that the connection had been terminated, but Jason was loathe to switch it off.

Just as the restored crops grew and developed, so did the relationship between Preeta and Jason. At long last the long-expected harvest arrived. The yield was in excess of what had been predicted, providing the Nivarna planets with their first bountiful supply of home grown fresh fruit.

As for Preeta and Jason, they worked their two farms together, barely being out of each other's company and happier than they'd ever been before.

CHAPTER 21

THE DAY OF THE NIGHT

The bright blue sky of a Nivarna 12 morning was obliterated by clouds of smoke and ash from the nearby volcanic activity. The air was thick with fine dust and the cloying smell of sulphur.

Jeff Kendale woke up, having to deal with an extended bladder. He noticed that the day wasn't as bright as it normally would have been at that time of the morning. When he returned to the bedroom he opened the curtains and was presented with a worrying vista: there were lava fields in every direction. He woke Connie his wife and she went to look out of a window that faced the rear of the farmhouse. They both realised that they had to leave the area as quickly as possible.

Connie began to collect and pack their important belongings, while Jeff went outside to see if the transport pod was functioning. He climbed inside and entered his identification code. No response. He tried again, in case he'd made a mistake, but that didn't improve the situation. Jeff realised that the control track must have been damaged, most likely by the encroaching lava. He went back inside and walked through to the kitchen where they kept the emergency response system. He switched it on and pressed the red emergency button.

Within a few seconds a voice responded. Jeff explained their situation and that the transport wasn't working. While he was speaking an anti-grav vehicle was dispatched to their location and would be with them as quickly as it could.

"You get all that you need out of your farmhouse and wait outside the front under the verandah. That will protect you from some of the falling debris."

"Thank you," Jeff replied, "we'll be ready for you."

Jeff switched the set off and went upstairs to the bedroom to help Connie with the packing. He collected together the official documents that they needed but he was sure that there would be those who either didn't have time to gather them or in the heat of the moment, they just forgot all about them. They realised that they couldn't take everything and a number of items were discarded to make it possible to fit what they had chosen into two bags each. Connie tried not to think about what was happening, but couldn't help shedding a few tears when she thought about leaving the house that had been her home for many years.

By the time the rescue vehicle arrived they were able to feel the heat that emanated from the lava, even though it was still quite a distance away.

"You two are in a bit of a pickle aren't you?" said the pilot, with a big grin on his face. "My mate and I will help you to get your bags packed and then we'll get out of here, before our feet get cooked." His light-hearted approach to what was an extremely dangerous situation helped Jeff and Connie to deal with what was taking place.

They finished packing the bags, along with a couple of other items such as the emergency communication system, the TV monitor, together with other computing devices placed into the craft, although other larger pieces (these used to be called 'white goods') had to be left behind due to their weight and size. Each farming couple would have to make similar decisions as their turn to leave their home arrived.

While this activity was taking place, the lava was getting ever closer.

"I think it's time for us to leave," said the pilot. "That lava is getting a little too close for comfort." Unknown to themselves, Jeff and Connie had been trying to drag their feet a little, not wishing to leave their home for the final time. Each one of them realised that they were sweating, due to their exertions packing items into the vehicle, but also due to the closeness of the lava.

They fitted themselves into the rescue craft, ensured that the doors were closed, clasped their seatbelts and the craft slowly began to lift into the air. The pilot could tell that the craft had a heavy payload, although it was able to deal with it without any difficulty. As they pulled away Connie could have taken one last look at the home she had shared with Jeff for all those years, but she wanted to remember it as it always had been, not as the conflagration caused as the lava took hold and burnt it to the ground.

As they headed towards the space port which, fortunately, was situated in one of the least affected areas of the planet, they could clearly see the devastation that had taken place across the majority of the agricultural land. The rare patches of green that still remained shone out like emeralds in a sea of dark, smoking, bubbling lava. As the realm of the lava expanded across the land the sky had taken on a dull red glow. What had once been a green and fertile planet, had now taken on a more primeval appearance, bearing little resemblance to the landscape that they were familiar with.

When the craft landed at the space port, the layer of ash on the ground could be heard crunching underneath it. Clearer areas, where other craft had stood, recalled a memory from the hidden recesses of Connie's mind. She was a little girl back on Earth. It had snowed overnight and as the vehicles were driven out of the parking area, they left similar patches that were clear of snow. The memory brought a smile to her face.

"What are you thinking about?" asked Jeff. Connie related her memory to him. "You've got a good memory," Jeff replied and looked out of the cabin window, "but I see exactly what you mean."

"I've never seen the snow!" admitted the pilot. "What's it like? I've heard that it's a really magical sight."

They continued their conversation as they exited the craft and made their way past the line of volunteers that were carrying Jeff and Connie's belongings from the craft to a place of safety, in a storage facility inside the building. As they entered the space port they drew in lung-fulls of the familiar smell. It was so nice to be in a place where the air didn't carry a tang of sulphur, but carried a mixture of the scent of catering, beer and other miscellaneous smells that a group of people create. They were each given a hot drink and sat down at a table.

"Tell me more about your memories of Earth," the pilot requested. It was a short conversation. The pilot had barely drunk half of his drink, when his communicator summoned his attention. He read the message and then said, "Sorry folks I have to go and collect another family. This is going to be a long run, so to use an old Earth expression, 'it's a foot to the floor job'! Anyhow, it's been a pleasure to meet the two of you and I hope everything works out well for you."

"Just before you go," Jeff asked, "what's going to happen to you? You're busy running about helping to save everyone, who's going to help you?"

"Thank you for asking. I'll be leaving on the final transport out, along with my trusty anti-grav craft. Don't worry, I'll be looked after. So far, you're the only one's who've asked that question. It's nice to know that I'm not taken for granted. I'll have to go, maybe we'll bump into each other some time. See you around." Then he was gone, off to save some other couple.

Jeff and Connie remembered how they felt when his craft appeared in the distance and felt reassured that others would be feeling the same sense of relief. They had just begun a conversation with a couple who farmed on the opposite side of the planet to themselves, when they saw Professor Lagardé who they knew by sight, though not personally, stand up on the platform at the end of the room.

"Ladies and gentlemen. The situation that we now find ourselves in, has on been on the cards for a long time. My team and myself abandoned the seismic research station a week ago, when we realised that there was nothing we could do to prevent the ultimate destruction of the planet. The current estimate gives the planet approximately two days only before the volcanic forces peak and destroy everything including the planet itself."

A murmur went through the gathering as they digested this information. As silence returned the professor continued.

"The first of the three transports, that belong to the Nivarna system, will be arriving in approximately one hour. This will be followed by the other two, to complete the evacuation. All the details of the evacuation were worked out some months ago when the plant's future was determined."

As this point the professor asked for a glass of water, as the sulphurous air was beginning to leach into the space port air system.

"If you look on your communicator screens, you will locate

the lists of the occupants for each of the transports. The three transports will allow you to disembark on Nivarna 9, 8 and 7, where accommodation will have been arranged for you. If you decide that you would prefer to permanently settle elsewhere, you will be free to do so. What has been arranged for you now is a temporary arrangement. I hope everything works out well for you all and that you all have a safe journey to your new homes and, finally, thank you for your attention."

Professor Lagardé placed the microphone on the floor and stepped off the platform as the audience briefly applauded. The space port became a hive of activity, which increased when the first transport craft arrived. By now everybody knew which craft they would be on and the correct people made their way to the departure gates at the appropriate time.

The farming community would be travelling on transports 1 and 2, with all the support staff, the seismic team and all of the valuable equipment, that couldn't be sacrificed, would be on transport 3, along with the anti-grav craft that had proved so invaluable. Their crews would actually be among the final humans to leave Nivarna 12 and there would be no return.

Following the departure of the first two transports, the last group had the space port to themselves, which actually helped to speed up their activities. The first tremor came as a real shock. It was so strong that a number of people lost their footing, causing a spate of injuries among those carrying the heavier items.

They were surprised by the violence of the tremor, although if they had been on the opposite side of the planet and had seen what had taken place, they would have understood. A large section of the planet's crust had broken free and sunk down into the underlying sea of magma. As the planet attempted to rebalance this catastrophe there were more tremors, accompanied by plumes of lava firing up into the sky. All the time other areas of the crust were being split apart as the planet entered its death throes, eventually to blow itself apart.

If an item, no matter how valuable or important, resisted its removal it was to be left behind. They just didn't have the time to spend on it. When the second and then the third tremors hit them, that was it. Professor Lagardé insisted that they load what had been removed onto the two anti-grav craft and then load themselves, along with their personal possessions. What was left had to be abandoned.

It should have been dark by now, the moons were plainly visible and the sky black. However, Nivarna 12 was never truly dark now, as the sky was swamped by a dull red glow from the volcanic activity that was taking place. It was now time to abandon the space port to its fate. As they made their way to the two craft another powerful tremor knocked some of them off their feet. Whatever had taken place caused a rain of ash to start falling, but what made it even more deadly was that there were small lumps of red-hot rock mixed in with the ash and a few of their number received rather nasty burns.

Professor Lagardé, along with a couple of members from his team, were the last to board the second craft. Both craft struggled a little to get off the ground, as they were overloaded, but they weren't going to ask someone to discard any of the payload. Slowly, but surely, they managed to lift off the ground, then gradually increase in speed. As they climbed higher they could see the extent of the volcanic incursion, the areas where the crust had succumbed, appearing as red wounds on the planet's surface.

Transport 3, like the two before it, was in a much lower orbit than it would have normally been allowed to attain. The exhaust from its propulsion engines was hardly going to corrupt the atmosphere any more than the planet was doing to itself. Anyway, a lower orbit gave the anti-grav craft a shorter journey to make from the surface. The crew of the each transport were astounded by the state of the planet and felt that everyone was fortunate to be able to escape. The crew of the transports were outstanding and did everything that they could to assist the Nivarna 12 refugees.

As the anti-grav craft travelled further away from the surface, they were able to appreciate the extent of the volcanic activity taking place on the surface. Although they were unable to feel or hear the tremors, they were able to see what was happening. Vast plumes of molten rock were being fired into the air, while rivers of lava made their way across what had been prime farmland. A number of the anti-grav passengers were making visual records as best they could. It was unlikely that they would ever experience anything like this again.

They felt a sense of relief as the transport came into view. The second craft waited, while the first attached itself to the airlock and then deployed the more substantial fixing clamps to secure it during the forthcoming journey. When the green light came on above the second airlock, the craft moved into position and made an airtight seal. The pilot lined up, using the instruments as he'd done a thousand times before. He thought he was secure, but the control panel indicated that a seal hadn't formed. So he tried again. Failure. After his third failed attempt, the transport pilot contacted him.

"Is everything all right down there?"

The pilot of the anti-grav craft explained what was happening.

"Well, it's been working all right up to now. It's obviously decided to start playing up at a most inopportune moment. Pull your craft away and come at it with more power than you would normally do."

Everyone already on the transport, along with those on the anti-grav craft, were getting worried. The clock was counting down towards the time the planet was due to explode and they wanted to be as far away as possible when that happened. The anti-grav craft hit the airlock so hard that everyone inside the transport felt it.

"Here goes," said the pilot. He manoeuvred his way through the docking procedure and this time, as they all waited with bated breath, the panel displayed a green light. The pilot attached the docking clamps, while everyone else scuttled through the hatch and once on board the transport, they waited for the pilot. He closed the anti-grav hatches and then sealed the transport's airlock door behind him.

"That was a bit dodgy, wasn't it? I've never had to hit an airlock that hard before and never want to again. I would think that the catches are well out of alignment now. A least we're safely inside."

"Thanks to you," someone said, followed by applause from the whole group. The pilot responded with a theatrical bow.

A member of the transport crew arrived and ushered them into the galley so that they could meet up with everybody else and watch what would happen to Nivarna 12. The pilot came on the intercom and announced that they would have to get underway at top speed as a great deal of time had been lost. An outside camera was trained on Nivarna 12 and fed through to the ship's monitors so that everyone could watch this once-in-a-lifetime event.

They'd been underway for about twenty-five minutes when Nivarna 12 finally disintegrated. No one on board had ever seen such a bright explosion before and could only imagine the noise such annihilation would make. The transport pilot wasn't paying any real attention to the blast. He'd hoped to be further away from the planet when it happened, even though he'd had the engines 'into the red' all the time. What concerned him was the pressure wave that the demise of Nivarna 12 would create. He'd never known a transport having to deal with a pressure wave before and didn't even know if it would survive the encounter. He could see the pressure wave heading towards them. The only possible course of action was to get as far away from the remains of Nivarna 12 as possible. He switched on the ship-wide intercom, explained the situation to everyone on board and told them to strap themselves in, or alternatively anchor themselves to something secure. He switched off the intercom, as the flight crew strapped themselves into their seats.

The pilot compared the image from the rear-facing camera with the radar image. They both told the same story. On went the intercom. "Brace yourselves, everyone – the pressure wave is just about to engulf us. Good luck to you all and I hope to see you afterwards."

Click. The intercom was switched off. The ship fell silent as they all pondered their fate.

CHAPTER 22

WHAT HAPPENS NOW?

Following the establishment of the Nivarna planets, Earth became a peaceful planet. Unfortunately, this peace was about to be shattered. Rumbles of dissension were growing throughout Earth's population. They wanted and deserved to know why the food supplies had been reduced. Various representatives of the authorities had tried to calm the situation down, with answers that ranged from the outlandish to complete lies. Such explanations didn't satisfy the populous. They were used to the ramblings of politicians and didn't believe a word they uttered. (At this time the authorities had not informed the population about the Nivarna planets' Declaration of Independence, which was the real cause for the shortage of food.)

The twenty-four hour news broadcasters sensed a big story and dispatched their investigative reporters. They were given the remit to dig up anything they could that would explain the current situation. In the following few days, brown envelopes of money changed hands (untraceable) and old misdemeanours were revisited, all to help numerous civil servants and politicians to change their mind and assist the reporters.

Their efforts were well rewarded. Two 'explosive' stories were uncovered. Following a preview of the material by the two station's commissioning editors, they both determined that the public had the right to view these stories, as they would explain the current situation and how the authorities were abusing their position. In an unprecedented move, the management of all the news channels were invited to meet together and view the two stories that had been discovered.

By now the authorities had learnt what the news channels were doing and the two stories that they were about to expose. So the authorities did what they always did when such a situation arose. They applied to the courts to suppress the material and prevent transmission. The application was heard in closed court conditions, with five judges, the recorder and the lawyers for each side. The lawyers employed by the authorities were able to twist and turn phrases so that they meant anything they wanted. The lawyers employed by the news channels were just as devious and it was difficult to believe that any of them knew what the truth was any more.

To start the case the judges wanted to see the material that was the subject of dispute. After viewing it the battle commenced. The trial continued on until the evening of transmission. While the judges retired to consider their decision the lawyers went to the bar. Upon the judges return they announced that the material was in the public interest and should be shown. Attempts by the authority's lawyers to raise objections were overruled. The judges' decision stood. They added that any attempts by the authorities to interfere with the transmission would be considered contempt of court. Then the appropriate members of the ruling government would be arrested and incarcerated.

While the court case was underway the news broadcasters made their plans. They came to a conclusion long before the court made its decision, which meant that if the judges decided in their favour they were ready to go.

The damaging footage had been combined into a 45 minute programme and they planned to transmit it continuously, in a loop, for a period of 24 hours. A unified approach like this hadn't been seen before, presenting everyone on the planet with the opportunity to see the material if they so wished. With all the news broadcasters working together, it presented a more difficult target for any saboteurs who intended to disrupt the broadcast. Once they heard that the judges' decision was in their favour, all the plans that had been made began to be acted on.

During the evening all of the entertainment channels mentioned the broadcast in their news bulletins, while the news broadcast channels deployed the extra security staff that had been taken on, 'just in case'. Emergency power generators were checked, along with anything else that might be 'got at'. Anything that could interrupt the broadcast was checked and checked again, while the clock counted down towards transmission.

The plan was to start transmission at midnight GMT, a standard recognised the world over. Then, as midnight progressed around the world, the broadcast would commence and then run for twenty-four hours. Even though many things had changed, there were still many cities around the world and they were all very similar, no matter where they were located. Once 23.30 arrived, the crowded streets began to empty and by the time the broadcast began the streets were almost deserted. This pattern was repeated, as midnight approached, even in the most remote islands of the world.

People watched the broadcast with a growing sense of disbelief that turned into anger. Some viewers watched the broadcast more than once, just to make sure that they had the contents firmly in their mind, while others made their own personal copies for future use once the broadcast was over. Regardless of the number of times people watched the material, or whether they copied it or not, the overall reaction was one of anger – anger at being treated in this way.

The first piece had been recorded a week before it was transmitted. It was never stated where it had originated from, although it could have been anywhere in the world. It portrayed a banquet for government members, along with their wives or partners, whichever was applicable. It appeared from the footage that it was recorded by a member of the serving staff wearing a hidden camera. This took place at a time when the same officials were urging the population to cut back as there wasn't the food available.

The second part of the programme was even more damming. Somehow, the reporter had managed to obtain an official recording made by the Nivarna Operating Committee which, unknown to the public, had been disbanded as it wasn't required any longer. This recording was of the meeting between the NOC and the delegates from the Nivarna planets. This was the meeting when the Nivarna planets declared independence from Earth and notified the NOC that they wouldn't be supplying any more food to Earth.

Now, the cat was out of the bag. Everyone knew why there

was a shortage of food and while people in general were struggling, the members of the authorities were living the high life and the better off of society were using the black market where possible. It wasn't surprising that the population of Earth were angry. Those who were supposed to take care of them were, in fact, exploiting them.

As midnight swept around the world it left behind it groups of irate people. The only place where this didn't take place was a small group of islands in the Pacific. Some years ago, they had decided to opt out of the electronic world that was engulfing society and return to the traditional way of life that their ancestors had lived for thousands of years. Their only concession was a radio on the largest island of the archipelago, just in case of emergency, but apart from that they carried on their lives as they always had done and were happier for it.

* * *

Looking out of her window, Carenza saw the people in the street below aimlessly milling about, occasionally stopping to talk to someone and then moving on. This was the situation that she had been waiting for. As she had grown older, Carenza had become more rebellious and, unknown to her, had come to the notice of the security service as someone to keep an eye on.

She prepared herself, tied her long copper-coloured hair into a ponytail, picked up her loud hailer and she was ready to go. As she walked into the mass of people nobody paid any attention, apart from a few women who looked admiringly at her hair and then smiled. There was a bench just across the road from her block of flats. As she stood up on the bench a few more people looked at her, but then moved on, not really knowing where they were heading. They needed a leader, someone brave enough to speak out for them.

When Carenza spoke into the loud hailer, their leader had appeared. "Why do we put up with this? We work hard to pay our taxes and then those who should know better waste every penny."

Now people were willing go stop and listen. Carenza continued speaking for a few more moments, not for too long so that the listeners were overwhelmed. This time, as she came to a halt, the crowd in front of her applauded, whistled and shouted in agreement. "You tell 'em girl!"

Carenza continued. "We should march to the government buildings and tell them how we feel. Will you join me?" A window shattering "Yes!" resounded from the crowd, as they began to move en masse.

They walked with a purpose now and began to sing some of the old protest songs from years ago, songs that the authorities had tried to stamp out. People that had gathered in the nearby area heard the commotion and saw the crowd moving as they passed the adjoining streets. When they saw that a leader had emerged they wanted to become part of what was taking place. As they moved toward the government buildings the amount of people kept growing as the streets joined together. All the time Carenza remained at the front, not on her own but part of an ever-growing crowd.

They weren't to know it, but others had followed Carenza's lead and had stepped forward to lead the crowd in their own part of New London. They all knew the security forces would be using the street cameras to monitor the situation, although there was little else they could do. If they moved in to remove the leaders, one of two things would happen: someone would immediately step into their place, or the extraction team might not get out of there alive, such was the antagonism of the crowd towards anyone who represented any part of the authorities. All they could do was watch, although they did plan to 'lift' the leaders after all this had died down, that's if the current regime survived.

The crowds from different parts of the city converged in Government Square. The security staff began to worry.

"This could become a full-scale riot if the situation isn't handled correctly," said Charlie, the senior security officer, "then we would be in real trouble." He turned to the sergeant who was in charge of communications and asked her to contact other security units around the country to find out if they had a similar situation in their area.

“I’ll contact the senator and ask him what he intends to do,” said Charlie. “After all, our orders will originate from him.” He removed his communicator from his tunic pocket and selected the senator’s office.

Ten minutes later he was knocking on the ornate oak door that was the entrance to the most exclusive and impressive room in the building. A weak “Come in” crept out of the room and Charlie entered.

“Hello Charlie,” the senator said, with a voice that was so quiet that it could have been a whisper.

“You can speak normally,” Charlie replied, “they can’t hear you, although I’d keep away from the windows if I were you. You just don’t know what might happen with a crowd like this, they’re in a volatile state.”

“What can I do?” the senator pleaded, his voice shaking. “How can I calm all these people down and persuade them to disperse? I just don’t know what to do!”

“I’m no diplomat,” Charlie replied, “but it would be a good idea to tell them the truth about what’s taking place and what the government intends to do about it.”

“That’s it,” the senator said, his voice much firmer now. “I have to explain to them and be blunt with them about what’s going on. Thanks Charlie, I knew that I could rely on you to get me out of trouble.”

“Let’s get everyone out of trouble, before we pat ourselves on the back,” replied Charlie. The senator sat down at his desk and used his communicator to speak to the technicians. He asked them to ensure that the PA screens were working, so that all of the assembled crowd were able to see and hear him, as he made his announcement to them.

Following his call, the senior technician said, “The old boy’s got some guts to go out there and face them. Let’s hope he survives. If he doesn’t, I don’t give much for our chances.”

While the senator was building up enough courage to step out onto the balcony, Charlie arrived back in the security office.

They all wanted to know what was happening. He outlined his conversation with the senator and then explained what he wanted them to do. They were to be positioned around the complex, just in case the crowd got out of hand and required restraining.

As they prepared themselves, Charlie walked over to Carice, the communications operative and asked her if she had managed to find out if large crowds had gathered at any other location. Charlie was surprised by the answer he received. It appeared that all over the world, crowds had started to gather following the conclusion of the broadcast. Charlie thanked Carice for her efforts and prepared to check on the deployment of the security staff. As he walked along one of the underground passageways, that linked the various governmental buildings together, he said to himself: I wonder if this is the beginning of a new world order?

At the front of the main building, which was the most ornate, there was a balcony just above the main doors. This was where important announcements were made from. As the government buildings covered a large area there were display screens mounted at strategic points all around the complex. This arrangement allowed members of the public to see and hear the announcement that was being made. When the screens flickered into life, the members of the assembled crowd knew that something was about to happen. The level of noise fell dramatically as this took place. Those at the front of the main building waited, their eyes fixed on the doors at the rear of the balcony. They were willing the doors to open, then they would be able to hear the excuse that the government would make this time.

The senator waited inside the doors, not wanting to step outside and face the crowd. His private secretary was attempting to instil some courage into him so he would step through the doors. "Come on Alfred. You know that you're going to have to do it eventually. Take a deep breath, take hold of the door handles and step out." Much to his surprise he did it and his secretary closed the doors behind him.

He was greeted by a cacophony of boos and catcalling. He

was able to cope with such a clamour; after all, he was a career politician and was used to such uproar being directed at him. He didn't attempt to speak, he just waited for the crowd to quieten down and eventually it began to. There were calls of, "Let him speak!" from different parts of the crowd. He felt that it was indeed now time to say something so he stepped forward to the front of the balcony.

"I've seen the same material as you did and I was shocked and disgusted by the content. I can assure you that neither I, nor any of my colleagues, were involved in any of those actions that have caused our present predicament. If I wasn't in the position that I'm in, I would have been part of the crowd that's in front of me now." This comment went down very well with the crowd. The senator was now becoming more confident, calling on the experience that he'd gathered over the years.

The senator waited for just the right amount of time, before he began speaking again. "The majority of those who have caused our current problems, were still in positions of authority in the government." Boos emanated from all parts of the crowd. "They have since been removed from their positions and sacked by the government and their state pensions cancelled." This statement brought a positive response from the crowd, in the shape of cheering and applause. The senator had to wait until the noise from the crowd died down. He didn't mind, he was getting into his stride now.

"As far the food situation is concerned," the crowd became silent, "I will convey to you all of the latest information that I have. As I'm sure you are aware, it isn't possible for the Earth to provide the amount of food that is required to feed the population that we have. That's why the Nivarna planets were brought on line. But, as you now know, the treatment of the farmers and other occupants of these planets eventually caused them to break off any contact with Earth. This has left us in the current dilemma, which certain officials kept covered up hoping that the situation would, somehow, sort itself out. But, of course, it hasn't and when everything came out, as it eventually would do, it came as a shock to everyone. As a result, all of you have gathered here and rightly demanded an explanation from the government."

He was doing well; they were listening to him and paying attention. "For some time now, government scientists have been trying to create synthetic food supplements to provide the essential vitamins and minerals that would normally be obtained from your food. Currently the final clinical trials are being conducted and it is hoped that full production can begin in the near future."

A mixture of murmuring and applause ran through the crowd and continued until the senator made his concluding comments.

"That's all that I can tell you. I realise that some of you don't relish the idea, but we have to deal with the situation we're in. Why don't you good folk go home now and get some rest. I've nothing else to tell you and there's nothing to be gained by remaining here. Even if the more rebellious ones among you decided to do your best to destroy these buildings, it wouldn't get you anywhere. The same situation would still exist, but the security services would be after you."

The edges of the crowd began to unravel and he felt satisfied that he'd managed to get through to them. He said a final, "Thank you for listening," to the crowd, turned around and walked back through the doors. As he entered his office his aide closed the doors behind him. The senator collapsed into his chair. He was exhausted. Three hours later the final members of the crowd drifted out of Government Square. Carenza's hour of glory was over, although she'd loved every moment of it.

Hidden away in the depths of the forest, in District 7, was the research centre that was conducting the clinical trials of the synthetic food supplements. The centre had four wards: two for the male volunteers and two for the female. The volunteers came from as wide an ethnic, genetic and physical mixture the scientists could locate. It was necessary to do this, to ensure that the supplements didn't have an adverse reaction on any particular group. There were just two weeks to run in these final clinical trials and everything was going well.

Right on time the night staff arrived from their dormitory

block. The previous shift completed the handover and then left the premises. All of the patients were seen by the nurses and provided with the last hot drink of the day, if they required one, along with anything else that was needed for the night, e.g. extra blankets. The whole building slowly quietened down as the patients fell asleep.

In his office Professor Lisburn was feeling very satisfied with life. He was day-dreaming about what the success of this project would do for his status among the scientific community, when the peace was shattered by the ward sister bursting through his door. He was so shocked by this, that he almost fell off his chair. She kept shouting the same thing over and over: "They're dead! They're all dead!"

Way above the satellites that were circling the Earth, the ever-present, ever-watchful alien craft was monitoring all this activity. When it monitored the events that had taken place in the research centre, it sent a simple two word message to the home planet. In translation: "It's started."

CHAPTER 23

"IS EVERYONE ALL RIGHT?"

As the pressure wave, caused by the explosion of Nivarna 12, engulfed Transport 3, it tossed the ship around like a matchstick. Unfortunately, three of the passengers broke free from their restraints and were thrown around the interior of the ship, breaking almost every bone in their bodies; the internal blood loss killing them all. The only other casualty was a lady from Nivarna 12's catering staff, who was hurt when a crate broke loose and fell onto her legs breaking them both.

After the pressure wave had passed by, the flight crew had the task of checking the craft's systems out and to establish if normal operation was possible. The pilot found that the positioning rockets would work and skilfully used them to stop the craft spinning end over end. The main problem for those on board was that the artificial gravity system had failed, so they all had to get used to moving about in a zero gravity situation. The main effect this had was felt in the galley, as the crew, along with some of the passengers, attempted to prepare some food and drink for everyone.

One of the ship's engineers did his best with some help from qualified staff, who had been part of Nivarna 12's technical support team. Following fifty minutes work, the artificial gravity system decided to work again much to the relief of everyone on board. Despite their best attempts the main propulsion system refused to operate, as did the flight deck control systems. The communication and navigating systems were part of the same circuitry, so they were also out of commission. As the internal communication system now functioned, after a fashion, the pilot was able to let everyone know what was happening.

It was rather noisy in the galley when the artificial gravity began to operate again. Crockery, cutlery, pots, pans and cooking utensils all threw themselves at the floor, taking various amounts of time, depending how close to the ceiling they had managed to get. Once the cacophony of sound had died away and their ears had returned to normal, they all found it much easier: now their food remained on the plate and for the chef's whatever they were cooking remained where they put it. It was also pleasant that hot drinks would remain in the mugs where they had been poured.

Following a thorough system's check the pilot was able to establish what would and wouldn't work. Armed with this information, he used the PA system to inform everyone on board: although they were safe and had plenty of food, they were unable to move or use the communication system to call for help. The only option open to them was to use the distress beacon and hope that the signal would be picked up and some help would be dispatched. The pilot also stated that it was a matter of concern that they didn't know if the distress beacon was actually working. He added that until help arrived, the engineers that they had would continue working to repair as many of the faulty systems as possible. "So if any passengers have an electrical engineering background, we'd be pleased if you would come and give us a hand."

The request produced three more engineers, each with a wide range of engineering expertise. It was fortunate that the ship was carrying all of the technical and maintenance staff that had taken care of the space port on Nivarna 12, which provided the widest spectrum of engineers possible. The main problem that they had to deal with was a lack of power. Some systems did function, but they were running on a secondary power buss. If they were able to re-establish the main power buss, then the major systems such as the flight deck instrumentation would begin to work again and they could establish where they were from the star charts. At the moment, even if they managed to get the main propulsion system functional, it wouldn't be a good idea to fire the engine, as they didn't know which way they were pointing. That's why the star charts were so important. At present, the best thing to do was to stay where they were rather than make the situation worse than it was.

At this point there were two things that the passengers and crew of Transport 3 weren't aware: firstly, that the distress beacon wasn't transmitting at full power, due to damage caused to the antenna during the ship's encounter with the pressure wave and, secondly, since it was realised that Transport 3 was missing, a search and rescue mission had been put together. This consisted of Transports 1 and 2, accompanied by a number of smaller craft from the Nivarna police force. The police ships may have been smaller in size, but they had a good turn of speed and were fitted out with a comprehensive array of electronic equipment, ideal for the mission they were asked to perform.

The engineers aboard Transport 3 had been divided into two teams: one was to try and establish power to the main communication system and the other was to attempt to reconnect the power circuits to the main propulsion system and the flight deck. One wasn't any real use without the other. It wasn't any use to have the engines working if you don't know where you were. One of the communication team, who had dealt with aerials in the past, volunteered to exit the ship and make a visual inspection of the array and establish that it was in working order. If anything was amiss he was qualified to make the required repairs. If his fellow engineers managed to persuade the transmitter to function correctly, it wouldn't be much use without the aerials being operational.

Fortunately, Matthew Tsenga had been part of the team that had developed the pulsed hyper-band transmission system that was used exclusively for distress beacon transmitters. He knew more about such systems and aerial configurations than anyone else aboard. He hadn't ever performed an aerial check under these circumstances, however, but was rather excited by the prospect.

Dressed in his EVA (extravehicular activity) suit, he checked the tools that were fixed to his suit and then tested his radio to ensure that the pilot's set was working, allowing them to converse. Once he was sure that everything was correct, he stepped into the airlock. The door was closed behind him and he turned on his air supply. Even though the air supply had already been checked he took one final look at the gauges. The system was filled to capacity, which he already knew, but wanted to check one more time before he stepped out into the void. One final thing to do before the door was opened, ensure that the safety strap was attached to the ship, which would prevent him drifting into space.

Matthew pressed the button to open the door to space and pumps started to remove the air from the airlock. He watched as the air pressure slowly decreased until it reached zero, when a red zero pressure indicator began to flash. It was now safe to open the door. Slowly it opened, revealing the velvet blackness of space, peppered with a magnificent display of stars. He stood at the edge of the exit, checked that his safety strap was secure and stepped out onto the side of the ship.

He'd chosen the airlock closest to the aerial arrays, although he still had to walk around a quarter of the ship's hull. As he started his journey, he occasionally stopped to admire the majestic sights that were presented to him. When the arrays began to appear above the curvature of the hull, he could immediately see a problem with the distress beacon antenna. During the encounter with the pressure wave, a lump of debris must have hit the aerial bending it over at almost a right-angle. It was so tempting to grab the aerial and bend it back into shape. As the aerial was 'live' he knew that he could not touch it. During the system development, a technician had made that mistake and the resultant shock had thrown him across the room.

On the flight deck, the pilot's conversation was interrupted by the handset radio.

"Hello, Bob, this is Matthew. Can you hear me?"

"Hearing you loud and clear. What can you see out there?"

"The main antenna array has come through our encounter with the pressure wave unscathed, but the distress beacon is damaged. It's bent over, causing the signal strength to be severely reduced. We dare not switch the transmitter off, just in case someone is looking for us, but it's very dangerous to touch it while it's live. Any suggestions?"

"Let me discuss it with my colleagues and then I'll get back to you."

While he waited for a reply, Matthew looked around, taking in everything that he could see. He loved being outside the ship and felt privileged to be able to see the vista that others couldn't. He took the dangers that were possible in his stride. A piece of debris, travelling at an incredible speed or a micro-meteor that happened to hit him were always a possibility, although the odds were against it occurring. It had happened in the past and it would happen again, it was one of the chances that working outside the ship entailed. The pilot had done a good job, using the thrusters to stop the ship turning from end to end, but it still slowly turned on its axis. It wouldn't be noticeable from inside the ship, although it would be seen from the flight deck.

"Matthew – are you there?"

"Yes, Bob, I'm still here. I haven't drifted off into space or anything."

"Very funny. Anyway, we've had a conflab and decided that the best course of action would be to attempt to straighten the aerial up. What do you think?"

"I had allowed for such a possibility when I put my kit together. I've a suitable rope to use for such an operation. You do realise that there is the possibility that the aerial could snap off. Such a procedure hasn't been performed in space before, with the aerial exposed to the extremely low temperature that it's now experiencing. Still want to go ahead with it?"

There was a pause before the answer came. "We've decided to give you the all-clear. If it snaps, we'll be no worse off, whereas if it's successful, the signal strength will increase dramatically. Good luck."

Matthew looked down into his tool pouch and carefully extracted the coiled up synthetic rope that was designed for such occasions. Without getting too close to the aerial he looped it around the bent section and closed the loop firmly around it. He had to be very careful, as the natural spring in the aerial fought against his efforts. Slowly, very slowly, the aerial began to straighten up. Then the rope slipped through the fingers of his space suit and began to flick about in slow motion due to the lack of gravity, as the aerial sprang back and forth. Had there been an atmosphere, he could imagine the sound it would have made.

Eventually it all calmed down. Matthew retrieved the end of the rope, but this time he wound it around his glove a number of times. After what seemed like an interminable amount of time, he took the pressure off the rope and stood back to admire his work. He was rather pleased with himself. The aerial was almost straight. This was the point where the temptation to just try to make it perfectly straight presented itself. Matthew knew from experience that it was best to leave well alone. He'd managed to get the aerial almost straight, which would improve the signal strength by a large factor and it was now time to withdraw.

He reported his success to the pilot and began the return journey to the airlock. As the outside door closed behind him, he was relieved to hear the air re-filing the airlock, so that he could enter the ship. Having spent the last hour in the vacuum of space, it took a while for his ears to adjust to all of the sounds that bombarded him as the inner airlock door opened.

As he was now under the influence of the ship's artificial gravity, the weight of the EVA suit caused him to move rather slowly, so he was glad that he was given some assistance to remove it. Matthew had always found EVA suits somewhat claustrophobic, so he was glad to leave the airlock area behind him, taking deep lung-fulls of air as he walked through the ship towards the cockpit.

One of the search ships was in the area where Transport 3 had drifted into, although it had been unable to pick up the signal from the distress beacon. As Matthew had straightened up the antenna, it was as if the signal suddenly appeared.

The Nivarna police craft sent a message to the search and rescue team. "I think we've found them!"

One of the other transport craft was close enough to join them and within a couple of hours the two craft came to a halt, facing the cockpit of Transport 3.

The passengers aboard T3 were busily engaging in passing the time, when they heard a ship-wide message from the pilot that changed everything. "The search team has found us! There are two rescue craft outside at the moment." The passengers started to gather their possessions together, not knowing whether it would be necessary to do so or not. What had been a quiet environment suddenly burst into life, with people moving from one place to another, each person totally engaged in their personal duties.

As radio communication wasn't possible, the police craft latched itself onto one of the Transport 3's airlocks. The visitor entered the ship in his police uniform. He received some strange looks as he walked through the ship, as the majority of the passengers had never seen a member of the Nivarna Police Force before. He began to smile as spontaneous applause broke out. The pilot opened the flight deck door to see what all the noise was about.

"Hello Andrew," the pilot said, "fancy meeting you out here!" The two old friends spent some time catching up with each others lives, as they walked into the flight deck, closing the door behind them.

Sometime later, the flight deck door opened and the police officer emerged. As he made his way towards the airlock, a number of the passengers asked him to tell them what was going on.

"Your pilot will be making an announcement in a little while." Everyone who asked him was given the same answer.

Before he left the ship, he went to see the lady who had endured the pain and discomfort of having two broken legs. During their conversation he established that her name was Nabeelah, although she was more commonly known as Nabby. He explained to her that all police ships engaged on a search and rescue mission had a doctor as a crew member.

"I'll inform the doctor of your situation the moment I return to our ship and then we'll prep the equipment he needs to make you as comfortable as possible."

True to the officer's word, the doctor appeared some fifteen minutes later and gave Nabby the pain relief she so desperately needed. He then placed her legs in temporary splints, the combination of these two treatments making her feel so comfortable that she actually dozed off. The doctor remained with her, monitoring her vital signs, etc, until they completed their journey.

While the doctor was treating her, the much-anticipated announcement was made by the pilot. “We have thoroughly discussed our options arriving at a unanimous and practical decision. We’re going to strap the two transport craft together, by whatever means our engineers can come up with. Then using the transport’s engines to move both craft along, we’ll make our way to Nivarna 7.”

None of those on board Transport 3 were expecting the celebratory welcome that awaited them, or how closely the whole Nivarna system had been following the reports about their rescue.

CHAPTER 24

DOWNHILL

Unfortunately, Saturday was an overcast day with intermittent rain and drizzle. This wasn't the type of weather a number of people were hoping for. Nevertheless, their plans were not going to be brought to a halt by a drop of rain. There were too many people who needed an opportunity to make their feelings known.

A number of cities around the world had experienced large-scale demonstrations, all based on the same complaint – the shortage of food. Up until now, District 1 (that used to be called the United Kingdom) had avoided such demonstrations, although the security services knew that they wouldn't be immune forever.

The security services were worried. The normal electronic chatter that they were able to monitor had almost ceased. They realised that the militant groups that provided them with some intelligence via their 'chatter' must have developed another way to communicate. As yet, all of their communication experts had been unable to unravel what system they were using.

When the wind was blowing in the right direction, the residents of New London were able to hear the chimes of Big Ben, which was part of the tourist experience that included the Houses of Parliament, which was the old seat of government and the area known as Whitehall. Tourists flocked to this location from all over the world. The majority of residents of New London, however, rarely visited, as it was seen as an ancient, irrelevant part of history.

As District 1's clocks indicated that midday had arrived, the situation in nine cities changed dramatically, catching the security services totally off-guard. Out of the side streets, rivers of people of all kinds appeared. Some with placards, groups supporting long banners, others with hooters, drums, in fact anything that would make a noise. As they made their way along what was obviously a pre-planned route, more and more people joined the crowd, the volume of sound they made increasing all the time. Then the chanting began.

The security service was in a state of panic. They weren't expecting anything like this; they had planned for the usual relatively quiet Saturday. Across District 1 there were requests for extra staff to report to security staff bases. This situation had caught them unawares, highlighting a serious flaw in their intelligence gathering arrangements. They amassed as many officers as they could, even calling some back out of retirement, in an attempt to make up the numbers.

Everything was going smoothly as the ever-growing crowd moved along the main streets, like some multi-coloured caterpillar. People on the streets cheered and whistled, showing their support in anyway that they could. The message of the demonstrators was one that currently affected everyone on Earth; except the rich and powerful, who always ensured that they were all right, regardless of what was happening to everyone else.

Although a number of demonstrations took place across District 1, the pattern of events was almost identical. The happy holiday atmosphere disappeared when the security staff appeared on the scene. Rather than maintaining a background presence, only becoming involved when required, they ploughed into the crowd attempting to arrest those that they perceived to be the ringleaders. Women and children started screaming and men tried to fight back. Try as they might, they were no match for the weaponry that the security staff were equipped with. What made the whole situation more dangerous was the attitude of the security staff themselves. They appeared to be under instructions to break-up the demonstrations, using any means at their disposal.

Left to their own devices, the demonstration would have eventually broken up, the participants fading away under their own steam, after having made their feelings known to those in charge – no harm done. As it was, a large number of people were in custody, including some members of the public who had tried to protect protesters from the vicious attacks by the security staff, or attempted to prevent them from being arrested and ended up being arrested themselves, receiving a beating for their trouble. People were running in all directions, some obviously injured, all desperate to get as far away from the security staff as they could.

Their task completed, the security staff faded away into the side streets, where their vehicles awaited ready to return them to their base.

The roads were covered in discarded placards, banners, shoes and a collection of accidentally lost items. A number of people lay on the roads, bleeding from a variety of wounds and miscellaneous injuries. Mixed in with this group of injured people were a few who had had the life beaten out of them, or who had died as a result of a number of differing confrontations. The scene looked like a battlefield. The medics walked between the bodies, assessing if there was anything that could be done to help any of them.

As the shortage of food became more severe, a normally law-abiding society began to break down. Any establishment that even hinted that food was on the premises was broken into and looted, not under cover of night, but brazenly during the daylight hours. By the time the security staff arrived, they were too late. All that they could do was pick up the pieces off the pavement and throw them through the broken windows. Eventually, as these break-ins became more commonplace, they didn't even bother to get out of the vehicles, as everyone had fled the scene, leaving litter strewn across the pavements, reducing the streets to filthy rubbish tips, which was accentuated as the situation continued to deteriorate and the population lost hope.

News quickly spread of a robbery that spread panic through the governing authorities, who thought that they were secure and safe living in their walled enclaves. Their food supplies were brought in to them by secure routes, or so they thought. A very well-organised group had hijacked the unmarked vehicles that were used to make the deliveries to warehouses where their contents were unloaded and then distributed into the enclaves.

The vehicles were stopped in a remote area and their drivers replaced with a gang member. The vehicles were then taken off-road into a quiet place where their loads could be removed without interruption. The drivers weren't harmed, but whatever threat had been made frightened them so much that none of them ever drove again.

This robbery of food from the high and mighty was the game changer that altered the situation for those in governance. They thought they were safe and protected but they now realised that was no longer the case. Their wealth and position were meaningless and they became determined to try and load the dice in their favour once again.

As the situation world-wide became more dire those placed in a position of overseeing the districts all around the world, began to realise that they were no longer able to manipulate the overall situation to their advantage. There wasn't anything they could do, apart from hoarding food for themselves and their compatriots.

They began to unburden themselves of anyone that they had the responsibility to feed: the first step was to empty the prisons, regardless of the crimes committed by the offenders. Questions concerning this move quickly surfaced from among their number.

"What if some of the more violent prisoners begin to kill members of the general population?"

"Think of the situation like this," came the answer. "It doesn't matter if people get killed or not. In fact, the sooner people die the better off they'll be and it will leave more food for the rest of us."

The food supplies that used to be allocated to the prisons found its way into the government clutches. They expected a backlash, but people were becoming weak from the lack of food and couldn't be bothered anymore. The schools were the next to feel the effects of the new plan and as the school was the only place where children were able to receive a good meal, the schools began to close down. The much reduced army (the other forces had been disbanded years earlier) whose only real task was to keep the population under control, although this task had mainly been assigned to the security staff these days, were the next to be disbanded.

The final nail in the coffin was hammered in when the health service was closed down. Local doctors tried to care for their patients as best they could, as did the hospitals, although they were overrun with patients suffering from malnutrition. Without food and vitamins to build their patients' strength up what could they do? Supplies of medicines had stopped, so even with judicious use of what they had, it couldn't last forever.

No one had paid any attention to their utility supplies, which by now were all ruining on automatic settings. But they wouldn't last indefinitely and eventually the power stations began to shut down. Once the electricity went off, a number of systems automatically switched over to generators. Even with the up-to-date power cells that were designed for such tasks, they would keep running for a while, but they were only designed for short-term use until the electricity came back on, which never happened.

After a month, the systems in each district began to shut down. Mankind was reduced to a Stone Age existence. Whatever animals that were either indigenous or domesticated, became fair game as hunting parties roamed the land. Life quickly reverted back to ancient ways, living off of wild berries and any meat that could be obtained, as the rule of law slowly broke down. Old attitudes returned when a squad from the now depleted security staff appeared on the scene. Everyone hid inside, leaving the streets deserted. One day a man emerged from a building and challenged the squad to shoot him, releasing him from his misery. They obliged!

Having seen this take place, people wondered why they were in hiding. At one time self-preservation would have been the primary object, but this one man's action brought them back to their senses. They began to emerge onto the streets and started to implore the security unit to terminate their lives. The security staff looked to their officer for guidance. He didn't know what to do, so they retreated. They were followed to the edge of the town, where they had left their vehicles, by a large crowd each and everyone pleading to be shot.

By this time it was commonplace to encounter bodies lying in the street. Often people already weak from lack of food, collapsed on the street, too frail to get up again. They died where they fell. When this situation began to develop, any bodies lying in the street were collected overnight and disposed of in large pits at the edge of the cities, towns or settlements, where people gathered. This service no longer took place. Wherever a person died, the body was left to rot. The Earth began to stink.

As the situation became more acute, families, especially those with young children, didn't want to experience their children dying of starvation, so they took drastic action. Wherever in the world they resided, they made use of whatever was on hand to commit suicide. The knowledge that their bodies would be left wherever they ended up didn't concern them any more: life and the daily suffering they endured, would be over once and for all.

Security squads across the world began to encounter people asking to be shot, so as to end their miserable lives. As they reported this situation, when they returned to their particular base, those in charge contacted the remains of the local government in their particular district. The response they all received was the same, regardless of the district. They were told to call all their units in and await an important announcement. The security staff that had already shrunk to half its original strength, was disbanded that day.

Once they heard that announcement, they roamed through the building searching for anything edible and resolving any outstanding grudges with a bullet. Once in a position where they could do as they pleased, they were now on the same level as the rest of the population, having to do the best that they could for their families. Whatever anyone did, wasn't going to do anything to stop the relentless march of starvation across the face of the Earth, leaving a trail of misery and death in its wake.

The remainder of the local government attempted to contact similar authorities in other districts, only to find that many of them had already disbanded. Unsure what their course of action should be, they decided to contact the central government, a move normally made only in extreme circumstances. They felt that the current situation qualified. They had to wait a while, as many other districts also sought guidance.

Eventually they received an answer – one that they weren't expecting. A recorded message conveyed its information:

"The central government has run its course. We are unable to rectify the current situation and save the Earth's population. We are, therefore, closing down at the end of the week and we suggest that you do the same. We thank you for your support and efforts, but there isn't anything that any of us can do to avert the developing situation."

At that the message signed off.

They looked at one another. "That's it then. What more can be said! Let's go up to the restaurant one final time and see if it's possible to make one last cup of coffee together and then make our way to our homes. All we can do is wait for the inevitable outcome."

For the first time in the aeons of earth's history, man was without any kind of government or law. If such a thing had occurred in the past, there would have been many people who would have taken advantage of the situation, whereas in the present climate people were either too weak or just couldn't be bothered anyway.

Then someone, somewhere, came up with a suggestion, one that shocked many people, even though they were in a weakened state.

"I've a better idea than to allow all these dead bodies to rot away and stink the place out. I'm sure that we could retrieve some meat from them. After all, they're going to waste anyway." Even though the communication networks had failed a long time ago, this idea somehow spread around the Earth.

Some accepted it gratefully, while others were repulsed by the idea, even if it was thought that following such a course would save them from starvation. Of course it didn't. Our digestive systems aren't designed for such a diet of flesh alone; to remain alive we require a balanced diet, which they weren't receiving. Death, either delayed or not, was inevitable under the current circumstances.

As mankind sank into the abyss of depravity, they'd reached the lowest point they could possible sink to. No doubt, in the desperate quest to keep alive, someone, somewhere, would come up with something else.

Try as they might, one thing was sure: mankind had squarely placed both feet on the downhill road that would eventually lead to extinction.

CHAPTER 25

"THEY'RE HERE!"

The occupants of the table closest to the entrance were carefully watching the activity in the space port's main corridor. Eventually their patience was rewarded. Officials suddenly increased in numbers. They'd never seen so many before. Maybe they all wanted to be part of this momentous occasion.

"I think they must have arrived," one woman said to her husband, speculating on the reason for the increase in activity.

This comment was overheard by those sitting at the adjacent table, which was only a couple of feet away. The original comment changed slightly by the time it had rippled, table by table, to the one occupied by Javan and the other farmers. The message that they heard was, "They have arrived".

They carried on the conversation that they had been involved in before it was interrupted by this speculative message. Javan's companions were more interested in finding out why he was on his own.

"Santos asked me to leave him at the farm today, as he wasn't feeling too well," Javan stated. "He's been doing that a lot recently."

"How old is he?"

"I've no idea, actually. Our individual ages have never come up for discussion, but he must be getting on a bit by now."

"That's what I was thinking. He has always been..." the comment was interrupted by the PA.

"Nivarna 7 is happy to announce the delayed arrival of Transport 3 from Nivarna 12."

People began to move about, as they prepared to leave the room and await the arrival of the passengers.

"I don't know why they're getting up. It'll be ages before the customs officers clear the passengers through arrivals," said Joe.

"After all," Bruno added, "those onboard Transport 3, were the last ones off Nivarna 12 before it exploded. Who knows what kit they were able to salvage."

“I think that they’ll get the passengers off first and then deal with everything else afterwards,” said Javan. “That’s the most logical way to approach the situation.”

“Who has ever known officials do things logically?” Bruno chipped in. They laughed.

Their speculation proved to be correct. The anti-grav ships could only bring a limited number of passengers and their personal possessions, on each trip from Transport 3. The pilots of the anti-grav ships always marvelled at the size of the transport craft. By the time they closed in on the airlock, it took over the sky, obliterating everything else.

As they returned to the surface, the pilot listened to the chatter of the passengers: “It will be lovely to breathe fresh air and feel the wind on my face,” said one. “Won’t it be nice to feel solid ground under your feet,” added another.

There were also many other similar comments, including many praising the pilot and crew of Transport 3, as they’d been looked after really well under extremely difficult circumstances.

The anti-grav pilot felt the tension grow among his passengers. Following the landing all chatter ceased; the passengers didn’t make a sound. When the door opened they all just sat there. The pilot remained in his seat and watched what was happening via his mirror. Eventually he said, “Come on ladies and gentleman, one of you has to be the first to make a move. Who’s it going to be then?” He got up out of his seat, walked through the passenger compartment passing them all and stepped out onto Nivarna 7.

Whatever it was that kept the passengers in their seats, was shattered when the pilot stepped out of the ship and onto the surface of Nivarna 7. They meekly followed the pilot, as he led them towards the customs and entry post. As they walked along they were sniffing the air, getting used to the odour of a new planet, as most of them had only been residents of Nivarna 12 since leaving Earth to begin a new career on a new planet. As the majority of the passengers had been Earth citizens, it took some time to establish their credentials as citizens of the Nivarna Planetary System. Fortunately, the customs official from Nivarna 8 and 9, who had dealt with many of ex-Nivarna 12 citizens who were on board Transports 1 and 2, were on hand to help out. With the extra assistance the passengers were all cleared by the time the second anti-grav craft landed with yet another group seeking refuge.

They were somewhat overwhelmed by the large numbers of people who were there to greet them, as they exited customs and were now officially citizens of the Nivarna system. They were led to a meeting room where they received a thorough medical check-up. This was to ensure their physical wellbeing and to check whether any had been exposed to any radiation during their sojourn among the stars. Cuts and scrapes were tended to, being cleaned and dressed as required. Then they were led into a re-arranged restaurant and offered a drink and meal, as that would have been one thing that wasn't available on Transport 3. The pilot and crew were also invited, as they'd been through the same ordeal as the passengers. Following their medical checks the crew joined the passengers in the restaurant. They were welcomed with a round of applause from the passengers, who were so grateful to have been brought safely to their destination.

Javan and co. were still sitting at the same table. The only change had been that during the interim period they'd been joined by Bruno's wife, Collette.

"I wanted to be on hand to welcome whoever it is that's been assigned to stay with us until they are able to sort themselves out," she stated.

Javan, Bruno and Joe were in the minority, most or those waiting to meet the passengers were the wives of farmers who were too busy in their fields to spend time waiting to meet their lodgers.

"I'll meet them when I've finished work and come home," was a statement made by many of them.

Having a manifest of Nivarna 12's occupants, at the time of evacuation, helped those assigned to work out the accommodation placements on Nivarna 7, 8 and 9. As Transports 1 and 2 had already delivered their passengers, a process of elimination provided a list of those on Transport 3, long before it was located and brought to its destination, Nivarna 7. This proved an invaluable aid when ensuring that the correct people were assigned to the most suitable family. In the majority of cases they chose well, although there were a few changes as would be expected.

Once the passengers had completed the first cooked meal that they'd had since leaving Nivarna 12, Transport 3's crew left, to assist in conveying the damaged craft to the base used for repairs and maintenance of those valuable assets of the Nivarna system.

When everything had settled down again, Hani, one of the space port's administrative staff, entered the room holding a collection of papers. When she had everyone's attention, she started. "We have spent a great deal of time and effort in preparing these assignments and, speaking on behalf of the team, we hope we've got it right. If things don't work out please let us know and we'll do all we can to change things around. Once the allocations have been announced, if you could make your way out into the main corridor and conduct your greetings there, then everyone else will be able to hear the remainder of the announcements!"

Santos and Javan's farm had presented them with a challenge, as they were the only all-male farm on the planet. So Professor Lagardé, the head of the seismology and volcanology team was assigned to stay with them. Javan was the first one at his table to receive an allocation, which surprised them all.

"See you around folks," he said as he stood up and went to meet the professor in the main corridor. Javan was rather pleased by the selection, looking forward to enjoying some enlightened, expansive discussions with the professor in the coming days.

Javan took the professor's personal bag and then led him to the transport pods' parking area. Once they were settled, Javan secured the code that would direct the pod to Santos's farm. As they started to move Professor Lagardé began to speak.

"I think that it would be a good idea if I introduced myself, as we'll be living in the same farmhouse. Call me André. Have you another name?"

"No, just Javan and the missing member of the team that you'll meet at the farm, is called Santos – Santos Memphis."

"That's an unusual name!"

"He's old enough to have been born during the period when it was the fashion to give a new baby an unusual name. Thankfully that fashion didn't last too long."

"What about your name – it's quite unusual, too?"

"That's a name I chose for myself, after my wife died and I left Earth. It's been with me ever since, in the many years that passed by that event."

The pod began to slow as it approached the farmhouse, coming to a halt alongside the verandah. When they'd disembarked the professor looked at the fields stretching to the horizon.

"This reminds me of a painting that my parents had on their wall; an actual oil painting, not a 3-D print like we have nowadays."

"I've never actually seen a real painting. I remember even in Earth's art galleries and museums, the walls were hung with 3-D prints. The real items were stored away somewhere, if they still existed, that is."

"That's why my parents' painting has stuck in my mind. The view was very similar to the one I'm looking at right now: a picture from the agricultural heartlands of France, when it existed."

Hearing voices at the front of the house, Santos came out to meet his houseguest.

"Santos," Javan said, "this is Professor André Lagardé."

Santos took a couple of steps forward and curtsied. As he stood up, he said, "I'm sorry that I don't have a posy to give you, your Majesty."

"That's all right, I'll forgive you this time," André replied.

There couldn't have been a better meeting between them all, a light-hearted, laughter-filled beginning to their relationship.

"Come through to the kitchen," Santos requested. "I've got a pot of stew bubbling. Sorry, but I haven't any French bread, we'll have to make do with what's available."

"That's fine by me," André replied. "If the bread is as good as the stew smells, I think we're in for quite a feast."

Once the meal was over and they were replete, the usual pattern took over. Javan cleared up the kitchen, while the other two were each armed with a mug of ale and sat out on the seats under the verandah to watch the sun go down. They were joined by Javan once he had finished his chores and then they spent the remainder of the evening getting to know one another.

The following day André was shown around the farm, together with demonstrations of all the computer-controlled equipment that was used. André marvelled at the ploughing array, enabling them to work the huge fields that were a feature of all the farms on Nivarna 7.

"When I compare your superb machinery with that on my grandparents' farm, the amount of engineering development is amazing!"

"All the kit we have was especially designed for the unique challenge presented to farmers on the Nivarna planets," replied Javan, really enjoying chatting to André. He'd been through so many different experiences and had visited so many different parts of the Earth. Not that Javan didn't enjoy talking to Santos, he did and always would, it's just that André and Santos were totally different people: each of them were so knowledgeable and capable in their own areas of expertise.

The next day they were informed that on the following Saturday night there would be a 'getting to know you' social gathering at the space port.

"I think I'll give that one a miss," announced Santos.

"It'll give you a chance to meet the other refugees from Nivarna 12," said André.

Santos's next statement really surprised Javan. "I just don't feel well enough to deal with something like that. I'll be overwhelmed by all those people. You two go and enjoy yourselves, just leave me out."

That was the first time Javan had ever heard Santos speak of feeling unwell. There had been times in the past when he thought that he wasn't too good, although Santos had never said it before.

Saturday night arrived and Santos had retired to his bed by the time that they were ready to leave. Javan quietly tapped on

Santos's door and then went into to ask if there was anything he needed before they left.

"No thank you, I'm fine." Santos replied, but he took Javan's hand and added, "You've always been very kind to me and have been the best friend a man could hope for. Off you go and have a good evening. Goodbye my friend."

Javan was taken aback by that comment. In fact, he had a sense of foreboding, brought on by the words, 'Goodbye my friend'. As Javan exited the room he almost bumped into André who was walking towards the front door.

"Is he all right?" he asked. "I overheard the last few words he said."

"I don't know," replied Javan, "I'm a little concerned about him. He's not a young man and he's had a hard life. So who knows what's going on with him? He'll most likely be up and about as normal in the morning – who knows."

"Would it be worthwhile getting a medic in to check him over?" André suggested.

"If you knew Santos as well as I do, you wouldn't even consider that," Javan replied. "He hates anything medical. When I first came to stay with him, I made that mistake one day. I received a verbal beating unlike anything I'd ever experienced before."

"Oh, I see," said André, with a smile on his face.

"Apparently, it was due to medical negligence that his wife died and since then he won't have anything to do with doctors, nurses or anything of a medical nature."

"That's quite understandable, under those circumstances," stated André, the smile having departed from his face.

Javan was very quiet as the transport port made its way towards the space port. The silence was finally broken by André.

"Are you worrying about Santos?"

A long pause followed. "Yes, I am," Javan replied. "Normally a comment like that wouldn't bother me at all, but when he made it this time, it left me feeling totally different."

"We can always turn around and return home," André suggested.

"No," Javan replied. "I think it would be better if we stick to our plans. If anything is going to happen, it will take place whether we're there or not!"

"Good point," André replied.

The space port reception for those from Nivarna 12 was well underway by the time Javan and André arrived.

"Would you like a drink?" André asked.

"That's very kind of you," Javan replied, "I'll see if I'm able to find somewhere for us to sit."

"Good idea, I'll see if I'm able to locate you," said André as he headed for the bar.

They both really enjoyed the evening. André became the professor once again, as that was how the Nivarna 12 citizens knew him. Javan introduced him to his fellow farmers and the professor reciprocated by introducing Javan to those that travelled with him on Transport 3, including his volcanology and seismology team. They in turn introduced Javan to the people who they were staying with, which was interesting for Javan as some of them were from the other side of the planet and he'd never met any of them.

Before they realised it, it was time to return home. The place started to empty as people began to drift away. Javan was on edge as they began the journey back to the farm. This time André decided to keep silent, leaving Javan to his thoughts and speculations. As the pod turned off the main track and began to speed up again for the final part of the journey, André could feel the tension building.

The moment they pulled up outside the farmhouse, Javan swung the lid back and leapt out. He was in the door before André had exited the pod. A few moments later he emerged.

"I quietly opened his bedroom door and Santos is sleeping like a baby. He seems to be okay." Javan's demeanour had changed dramatically. He'd reverted into the person that André was getting to know. They both felt so tired, following their evening out and the amount of ale they'd both consumed, they could only manage the briefest 'goodnights' as they made their way to the bedrooms. Javan was worn out, physically and mentally following the stress caused by worrying about Santos, and the evening out. He didn't bother to get changed. Slipping his shoes off, he slid in under a blanket and was asleep before his head touched the pillow.

Javan was woken-up the next morning by the rap of knuckles on his door.

"Come on, it's time to get up! Breakfast's ready." It was Santos's voice and he heard him repeat the same message on André's door. It was a struggle, but Javan and André both made it into the kitchen. Santos seemed exceedingly bright that morning, almost a little too good to be true. The coffee and warm food began to wake them both up, so that by the time breakfast was completed they were wide awake and ready to face the day. As a thank you for all that he'd done that morning, Javan and André cleared the table and prepared to start the washing up.

"No you don't," said Santos. "You go and get yourselves ready for the day."

Jason and André looked at each other, unsure as to what was going on. Javan was especially suspicious. He'd never seen Santos like this before in all the years he had known him.

Three days later, Santos died. Javan had prepared breakfast and had knocked on Santos's door, but didn't receive a reply. In case he wasn't feeling well, he cautiously opened the door and stuck his head into the room. He couldn't hear him breathing. He then stood and watched Santos lying in his bed. Plucking up his courage, he reached out to feel for a pulse in his neck. The moment he made contact with Santos's neck he recoiled. He was stone cold. He left the room, quietly closing the door behind him.

Javan knocked on André's door. Fortunately he was already awake.

"Come in," he answered. Javan walked in. "Whatever is the matter? You're as white as a ghost."

"Santos is dead." He felt tears running down his cheek and brushed them away with the back of his hand.

"Take the weight off your feet. Sit down on the bed, while I go and check him out."

“Thanks,” Javan replied.

He heard André enter Santos’s room and then a few moments later he heard the door close.

André re-entered the room. “I’m afraid that you’re correct,” he stated. “I presume that you have the same medical situation procedure as we had on Nivarna 12?”

“Yes, I think it’s standard throughout the Nivarna system.”

“I would be happy to do it, but as a newcomer they wouldn’t know who I am, so I’m afraid that it’s all going to fall on your shoulders.”

Javan’s head was in a whirl. Experiencing Santos’s death brought back memories of dealing with his wife’s demise, all those years ago. The memories were still as acute and bitter as they had always been. It was fortunate that he was on his own as he began to cry, a real sobbing cry, an outlet for all that he’d been holding in for so many years. He went over to the sink and splashed his face with cold water, then patted it dry. Then he walked over to the worktop, where the communicator base unit was fitted. He pressed the red ‘emergency call’ button and received an almost instantaneous answer. He explained the situation to the female operator, who transferred him to the appropriate team.

“Have you moved anything?” the man asked.

“No. Once I realised that he was dead, I left the room and closed the door behind me.”

“That’s good. It’s best that we encounter the scene as it was at the time. We’ll have a team with you within the hour. Now take care of yourself and if you want to cry, let it all out.”

“I know that’s best,” Javan replied. “I was given the same advice when my wife died during an accident back on Earth many years ago.”

The gathering to say farewell to Santos was held at the space port. Javan was surprised by the number of people that attended the occasion. There were representatives from each of the other Nivarna planets, along with personal friends that Santos had encountered over the years, many of whom he’d got to know at the system gathering, when the decision was made to push for independence from Earth. Javan found out that Santos and his wife were two of the very first settlers on Nivarna 7 and, as such, always had a special status. He was one of the few members of this exclusive group that had died and was part of the beginning of the reduction of the population of the Nivarna system that would accelerate as the years passed by. For Nivarna 7, it was the end of an era.

CHAPTER 26

HANDOVER

The conclusion of all industrial processes, along with the continuing reduction of the human population, was giving planet Earth a chance to begin to recover from the assault it had been under for many years. It was much quieter and the air was much cleaner than it had ever been since the beginning of the Industrial Revolution. None of the improvements that were taking place were noticed by those still alive. They were more concerned with survival, although they realised that their chances were not good.

All of the built-up areas had been abandoned. There wasn't anything left to eat in any of them; also there were marauding bands who sought out the unwary in such places and would rob them of anything of any value they had, often killing them in the process.

Many had taken to living in the countryside forming shelters out of natural materials that blended into the surrounding features. Although they had the ability to light a fire they wouldn't dare. The plume of smoke and its aroma would give away their location to the cannibal groups that roamed the land in a never-ending search for fresh meat. The lack of a fire was tolerable during the warmer months, but as the winter approached they found it increasingly difficult to resist the desire to warm themselves despite the danger they put themselves in.

On a still cold night, one group was woken by screams coming from a nearby family who had lit a fire to keep themselves warm during the night. The lack of a good diet caused the body's condition to deteriorate and remaining warm on a bitter winter's night became almost impossible. The screams were soon over. Those that had been caught out didn't have to worry about staying alive any longer. Their deaths meant that others could sleep soundly as the cannibal group would be sated by their activities and wouldn't emerge from their victims' shelter until the following evening.

There were a number of people who managed to avoid such threats to their continued existence. When they had seen the way things were going, they'd moved out into the wilderness areas living solitary lives not unlike medieval hermits.

There were those who had information concerning the whereabouts of fully-fitted out shelters. These had been constructed in the days of impending threat and had been maintained out of government funds each year. Attempting to gain access to one of these shelters would quickly demonstrate who your friends were. Most of those who hoped to be allowed in were left outside by those higher up the chain of command, who felt that they were more worthy of saving.

The majority of people didn't have access to such facilities and in a way were glad. Being enclosed and confined in a small underground area wasn't most people's idea of 'sanctuary'. How long would it be before arguments started? Then cliques would form. Would you be part of the correct group? Before long there would be the emergency of those who couldn't stand the confinement, becoming 'stir-crazy' and planning to do all they could to get the door open, a contingency that wouldn't be entertained by those in charge, and at that point the upset and dissent would really begin. Anywhere would be better than being shut in a shelter with a group of people that you didn't really like, never knowing who was liable to turn on you at any moment.

Compare that scenario to being deep in the countryside, breathing in the fresh air, enjoying the wild flowers and the sunlight. Of course it wasn't possible, or sensible, to sit outside in the winter months. Not only was it cold, but care had to be taken not to leave footprints in the snow or on the frosty grass.

Those humans brave enough to live in the most desolate areas of their districts had chosen many unique places to call home. Shelters and burial mounds left by ancient occupants were choice locations along with some very distinctive 'homes' that reflected the personalities of their constructers.

Once they had taken up residence and checked out the 'lay of the land' to ensure that they'd made a correct decision, they settled in, planning on long-term occupation. To begin with they often saw other people moving about in the landscape, but over time that number slowly decreased as age, predation and the inability to cope with their choice of lifestyle, took their toll.

There was a new phenomenon that shook the beliefs of many with space travel being commonplace, along with the development of the Nivarna planets. Most people didn't believe in UFOs, although there was a hardcore of believers who felt that humans were not alone. A number of the wilderness occupants spent the summer and autumn evenings watching the world go by. No one knows who was the first to see the large strange-looking craft that flew over the terrain always remaining at the same altitude as it mirrored the contours of the land.

They watched out for it each evening, those who were able, using the stars as a guide to when it would appear. As it came into view, it was always a little closer or further away each time, causing some of the more able to come to the conclusion that the Earth was being mapped. The purpose of this wasn't obvious, but various theories were considered. Without anyone to discuss these with, some outlandish conclusions were reached and others more likely close to the truth came to the surface. Everyone who saw the ship now believed in UFOs: they'd seen one for themselves.

While this was taking place a new threat to the remnants of humankind was preparing itself for an onslaught on those still living. Whether it was an old pathogen that had re-emerged, or a totally new disease, wasn't known. After all, there weren't any technicians anymore, or laboratories for them to work in if there were. No one realised what had killed the first victims. They were left lying where they fell, looking like anyone else who had died. The pathogen then found a new home in the cannibals who devoured the flesh of these corpses and so it began to spread across the land. Strangely, this pathogen appeared all by itself and infected the whole globe at almost the same time, no doubt due to the similarity in the conditions in each location.

Mankind was rapidly approaching extinction. In what had been urban areas, with populations of hundreds of thousands, were now deserted; the overall population of each district (as designated by the world government) could have been counted in the hundreds. Just to add to the decimation, the pathogen that had caused so many deaths had quickly mutated into an infection that was airborne and now produced visual evidence of infection.

As with the previous developments, wherever in the world you looked the situation was the same. The continent previously known as Africa was totally deserted, apart from a few individuals who had removed themselves from the general population. How long these would last was unknown. The chances of sustained survival weren't good for any of humankind who had survived up to that point.

As time passed, those who had managed to elude capture by one of the cannibal groups began to succumb to the effects of malnutrition and old age, that's if they'd managed to avoid contact with the new more virulent form of the pathogen. Everything seemed to be against humans remaining alive, or maybe it was payback for all the abuse the Earth had suffered at man's hands, that had created the conditions that were now causing its demise.

With the dramatic eradication of the human population, the cannibal groups found it more and more difficult to locate their prey. Any corpses that they came across were usually so putrid that even they wouldn't touch them. So the different groups turned upon one another, further speeding up the process of extinction.

It didn't take very long before the only humans left were those who had removed themselves from the social groups and relocated to the wilder areas of their particular district. They didn't realise it at the time they made the decision that their choice had prolonged their lives. The pathogen that had ravaged the population died out in cold conditions and as their choice of habitat was in the remote, cooler areas, they had escaped its worst effects.

They noticed, as time went by, that fewer people could be seen moving about in the landscape. Eventually the situation arrived that they had to assume that they were the only ones left. Was that a valid conclusion? Were there others, who had made the same choice as themselves? They wouldn't even know. At least they'd survived longer than anyone else, or so it seemed. Then they began to question their decision.

"Do I want to be alone for the remainder of my days?"

At this point some of them gave up and ventured back towards what had been the populated areas. The pathogen was waiting for them and quickly they were overwhelmed.

The few that remained were determined to sit it out. Whether they were on their own or not, they didn't know, or care, so long as they were able to eke out a meagre living and occupy themselves each day. There were a number around the globe who were also experiencing similar thought processes, each one asking themselves the same searching questions. One decision they all came to was that they weren't going to give up. If this was it until they died, so be it. That's what happened. One by one they began to die off, precipitated by illness, starvation or, in most cases, simply old age.

As the conclusion of the human era rapidly approached, human history didn't matter anymore. All of the developments and technological advancements had, by now, been abandoned. This included all the various type of spacecraft, which had allowed the establishment of colonies on other planets and then later on the array of Nivarna planets, to provide food for the ever-increasing population. All of these craft had been left at the reception and maintenance facilities on the moon. There they awaited their fate, as did the large space station parked at the Lagrange point between the Earth and moon. Planet Earth was now experiencing the twilight of humankind.

The rays from the early morning sun began warming the Earth, preparing it for another day, although it was unable to warm the body of the final human on Earth who had died during the night. The cause was never determined, as there wasn't anyone else alive to ascertain the reason. The woman had lived alone for many years, never knowing if she would ever meet another person again. In her travels she'd come across many corpses, lying where they fell, as no one bothered to bury them anymore. The appearance of some of the corpses had puzzled her. They looked as if they'd been ravaged by a wild animal. But there weren't any wild animals anymore, they'd been killed for food early on. After hours spent in thought, she came to the horrifying conclusion that some humans had reverted to cannibalism in an attempt to remain alive.

Not knowing that the cannibals had also died out a long time before, she no longer ventured down to the lower levels where the mutilated corpses had been found.

Now, she, too, had succumbed to the great leveller and her corpse would join all the others until the elements eventually disposed of her remains, to the benefit of many various types of micro-organisms. The date of this momentous occasion? It was Friday, 3rd May 2497, which heralded the conclusion of Earth's occupation by the human race.

Another species, however, had been patiently waiting for their chance to occupy the planet. They just had to wait until the humans had self-exterminated.

The following passage is a translation of a conversation that took place on the bridge of the alien flagship, some seven months following the demise of the last human:

"Well, captain, your theory worked out exactly as you said it would."

"Thank you, Sir. After studying the humans I realised that if their infrastructure was placed in a self-destruct situation, they would soon descend into a condition where self-preservation would override everything else and they would eventually destroy themselves."

"And that's obviously what has taken place."

"That's correct, Sir. Fortunately, we are physically quite similar to the humans, so four volunteers were surgically altered so that they could live among the humans and perform a variety of sabotage operations that would stir things up. Then all that was required was to leave the humans to get on with it, until they eventually arrived at the point where they sealed their own fate."

“What I like about this whole operation, captain, is the planet’s infrastructure has only suffered minimal damage and we haven’t had to spend a fortune on armaments.”

“Neither have we lost any of our soldiers along the way.”

“One negative point, that we should not overlook, captain, is the loss of our holy planet of pilgrimage, which they called... what was it?”

“Nivarna 12, I believe.”

“Thank you, that sounds about right. If only the humans hadn’t removed the stabilisation control it would have still been here. I suppose it’s a minor loss, seeing that we’re gaining a whole planet.”

“When do the authorities plan on re-populating what the humans called Earth, Sir?”

“We’ll send the first ship of clean-up squadrons in 6 kquans (a kquan= 5 days) and then build up the various teams until the planet is ready for habitation, then the civilians would be able to begin moving in.”

“Do we know what the planet is to be called, Sir?”

“That hasn’t been decided yet, but it will be confirmed before re-population commences.”

Earth’s new tenants were moving in.

CHAPTER 27

ONE WAY, OR ANOTHER

A large explosion in the engine room of Explorer 1 heralded the demise of the temporal distortion drive. It had operated surprisingly well, seeing that it was only a prototype. As the engine ceased to function, the field that encased the ship and caused all within to lose consciousness, slowly dissipated.

Explorer 1's occupants began to stir, taking varying periods of time to regain consciousness. There were a few who struggled to come out of their induced state and they were transferred to the ship's hospital, where Dr McAndrew accompanied by his nursing staff, coaxed them into recovery.

It took less than an hour before everyone returned to normality. By then the ship was buzzing with activity. The flight engineer had taken a couple of engineers with her to inspect what had taken place in the engine room. Following examination it was determined that the TD drive had burnt out and was beyond repair. Although the propulsion drive appeared to be serviceable they were unable to test it, as it was controlled from the pilot's position on the flight deck. So until the technicians working in that area were able to repair the damage that had occurred to the control system circuits, no one was going anywhere.

The catering staff had thoughtfully provided a hot drink for anyone who needed it and soon had a variety of snacks available. While this was taking place the head chef was recording all the food stocks in the pantry and store cupboards. He realised that the amount of provisions that had been placed on the ship indicated that the government had a much longer trip planned for Explorer 1, had the inaugural flight to Nivarna 12 been a success, but they would never know now as they appeared to be an inordinate distance from the Nivarna planets. Those on board, however, would be thankful for the food.

The technical support team had located a complete set of control system parts that were needed for the panels on the flight deck. As this was a comparatively small area, three technicians could just about manage to work there at the same time, although it was a squeeze. Once all the panels had been released and lifted out of their housings, it became impossible for all of them to work in there at the same time. The only solution was to leave the flight deck door wide open, then the electrician outside could collect the old parts as they were released and hand replacements to the technician who was able to fit them.

After four and a half hours of intensive work, all of the faulty parts had been replaced and it was then the moment of truth. The power breaker was operated and power to the panels surged through the systems. Rather annoyingly, everything came on except for one of the visual displays that was part of the navigational system. When this happened, words that aren't part of the usual technician's vocabulary were uttered. The power was switched off again and the faulty panel removed. By delving into the innards of the housing, a wiring connector had been pulled out when the panel was first removed. This connection was re-made, the panel replaced and fixed into position.

The power was switched back on. Thankfully this time all of the operating panels and the displays came to life. The technicians performed a few basic checks to establish that everything appeared to be functioning correctly and then cleared the area of all of their rubbish, which mainly consisted of the packaging from the replacement parts.

While this was taking place a junior technician went to search for the pilot to inform him that the flight deck systems were once more operating correctly. He was finally located fast asleep in his cabin, the co-pilot was similarly occupied in the adjacent cabin. Both were roused from their slumbers and a few moments later made their way to the flight deck, via the canteen to obtain a mug of coffee and a sandwich.

When they arrived at the flight deck, Bernice was already there, checking her engineering panel. She wanted to ascertain the situation with regard to the propulsion engine: whether it would work, how much fuel they had and how long that would last under varying circumstances.

“Where did you get that food from?” were her first words to the pilots.

“We picked it up at the canteen, on the way through,” came the innocent reply.

“Where were you then?”

“In our cabins, having a nap.”

“You lazy so-and-sos. I was up to my elbows in dust and debris from the burnt-out section of the TD drive, then I checked out the propulsion system and all the time I was engaged in that, you two were sleeping – typical men!”

While the co-pilot went back to the canteen to get coffee and food for Bernice, the pilot was busy re-adjusting his chair so that it was in the position he found most comfortable.

“I bet it was those technicians that moved it,” he muttered.

“If the technicians hadn’t been in here, your ship would still be broken. So having to adjust your chair isn’t a big price to pay, is it?” Bernice replied.

When Mike returned with Bernice’s coffee and food, the three of them settled into running through the test sequences that checked out each of the ship’s systems. It appeared that everything was functioning correctly. The only way forward now was to test out the two propulsion engines. The pilot realised that they needed to inform those on board about what was about to take place and avoid creating panic.

The public address screens came to life displaying a head and shoulders image of the pilot. “In a few moments you will hear some unfamiliar noises and hopefully feel the ship begin to move. If those tests are successful then all the department heads will meet together to be briefed on our current situation. Following this meeting, we’ll all get together in the main atrium and have an all-inclusive discussion with the intention of arriving at a consensus about our course of action. So, first of all, we have to test our only means of propulsion and if that test is successful then we can move forward, if not we’ll have to re-think our options.” The pilot’s face was replaced on screen by an image being received via a front-facing camera.

The majority of activity in the ship ceased as they waited to see what would take place. The next few moments would decide their future. They first felt a silent vibration in the floor, which grew in intensity, then was augmented by a roaring noise from the rear of the ship. Looking at the monitors they could see that the ship was slowly moving forward and as the thrust from the engines increased, so did their forward movement. When it was realised that they weren't going to spend the remainder of their days drifting in space, everyone burst into spontaneous applause.

When the engine was cut, the silence was almost oppressive. Some of them noticed from the monitors, that their forward motion continued and those who didn't know how this was possible had it explained to them.

The heads of the various departments were seen to enter the meeting room that was situated close to the flight deck, to discuss the implications of the satisfactory burn by the engines.

About half an hour later the pilot's image appeared on the monitors once again. "If it's possible for you to leave what you're doing at the moment, your presence would be appreciated in the atrium, so that we can decide our next course of action. Thank you." As Ranjit concluded the announcement, he wondered how long it would take before they all assembled together.

The ship came alive once again. The catering staff hadn't been so busy for a while as they provided drinks and snacks to the ship's company as they gathered for one of the most important discussions they would ever have.

The meeting was ready to get underway. Oversight of the meeting was to be by Bernice Heckt, the ship's engineer. There was no much chatter and noise from the attendees that conventional methods failed to gain their attention. Bernice took a slightly unusual approach to solve the problem. She placed a couple of fingers in her mouth and emitted the loudest whistle that anyone had ever heard. Such was the effect of this that a number of people 'jumped' at the sound, but it achieved the desired result.

"Thank you for your attention," Bernice said. "First of all, our pilot and co-pilot have been studying the navigational arrays and would now like to inform you of what they have been able to decipher. I'd like to hand over to Ranjit and Mike."

Mike, the co-pilot, was the first to speak. "From the outset, I'll let you know that we don't have any idea where we are. We do not know how long the temporal distortion drive was running, or the amount of distance we covered before the engine self-destructed. If we're honest, we could be in a different galaxy. Our star charts are totally useless, as they don't bear any similarity to the area where we're located. I'm sure that's cheered you up no end, so to discuss something more positive, I'd like to hand over to our pilot, Ranjit." Mike sat down. There was some spurious clapping, but all in all most of the audience were stunned by what he'd said.

Ranjit took over, spending a few moments scanning his audience. "Dear, oh dear," he said, "you're not the happiest looking audience that I've spoken to. I'm sure that a lot of what Mike had to say came as a shock to many of you. Actually, it's not all doom and gloom and I'll tell you why. We've two choices in front of us at the moment and the decision of which to choose is down to you. You'll have both options put to you and then you'll have some time to discuss the two scenarios among yourselves. If any questions arise, we'll be here to answer them for you."

The co-pilot, Mike Kirkwood, stood up to explain the two alternatives, enabling those on board to make a choice. He began in this fashion. "Okay, folks. It's decision time." He was trying to keep things as light as possible and not emphasising the seriousness of the situation. "As far as we've been able to ascertain from the navigation array, there is a solar system directly in front of us. One planet, the fourth, looks favourable but we won't really be sure until we're much closer. If it's not, we can then use the propulsion engines, with their limited supply of fuel, to find somewhere else. The second scenario: to forget about this system and move straight into search mode, looking further afield. None of us have any knowledge as to what's out there, or what we may find. I ask you to bear in mind, when deciding your individual choice, the fuel situation: once it's gone, it's gone. We don't have any reserves, or any other way of re-fuelling our engines. So that's it. They are the two options that you have to choose between. We'll take a break for an hour now, to enable you to discuss the situation with as many people as you want, while you enjoy a hot drink and a snack. I will join the other members of the flight crew along with the department heads in the canteen area. If you have any questions, or need something explained, feel free to come and speak to us. To enable us to reach a decision, we'll revert to a tried and trusted system. Each of you will be given a slip of paper, on which you may mark your preference and then place it in a sealed box. When everyone has made their choice the slips will be counted up and either choice 1 or 2 will be the course of action we follow. We'll all meet up again in an hour's time. Thank you for your attention."

As the hour progressed the noise level slowly grew, as the discussions gradually increased in volume and intensity. Occasionally there were some rather heated outbursts, although they were only brief interludes. The majority of the discussions were conducted in a good-hearted manner. The senior staff members were somewhat surprised by the number and variety of questions that were put to them. Fortunately, they were able to provide satisfactory answers even though a couple of them had to consult together. By the time the hour was concluded each and every one of them had reached a decision that they were content with.

The voting was concluded and the slips counted. Ranjit, as the senior officer on board, stood up to announce the result. "It's a very clearly split decision," he stated. "Sixty-eight per cent of you have chosen to check out the planet closest to us first, which means thirty-two per cent of you wanted to look further afield."

Those whose choice had been successful applauded. Ranjit raised his hand, the applause died away. "The choice has been made. Some of you were bound to be disappointed, whichever way the vote went, so let's all work together and go see what we can find."

CHAPTER 28

A POSSIBLE SOLUTION

Both propulsion engines had achieved maximum thrust, causing Explorer 1 to take on the appearance of a large Roman candle, as it attempted to light up the inky blackness of space while heading towards an unknown solar system.

Once the planned speed had been attained the engines were switched off, although the inner core of each unit was kept warm which kept the engine ready for the next time it was required. Coasting through space like this was the most economical use of their limited fuel supplies and it also had the benefit of stopping the vibration that the engines sent throughout the ship. Coasting had the downside in that the engines sounded that much louder when they commenced once again.

TV monitors, spread throughout the ship, were displaying a view of the area that they were heading for. It took three or four days before it was possible to notice a change to the image. The target solar system was becoming more defined and stars that had been a regular presence at the edge of the screen had disappeared. More attention and speculation began to be shown as they reached the point where individual planets could be identified; most of them had names given to them, each group of workers choosing their own.

As Explorer 1 closed in on the planet of choice, it appeared that the ship was going too fast, but they needn't have worried. The flight crew knew exactly what they were doing. Flying on this specific course, they had located what they were looking for between the planets and the largest of the four moons, finally carefully manipulating their position until Explorer 1 was parked in the Lagrange point. (The Lagrange point is the null point between the gravity fields of two planetary bodies, where the gravitational pull ceases to exist, so anything placed in that position won't move.) The flight crew had managed to place Explorer 1 in a position, where they didn't have to worry about remaining in orbit and thus using fuel, to avoid dropping into the atmosphere.

The pilot's face took over from a planetary scene on the monitor and explained that the planned provisional exploration was to be undertaken by one of the two modified anti-gravity craft that were stowed on board.

"Following the return of the craft, the pilot will meet with us all in the main hall to explain the results of the tests he was able to perform. We don't know what's down there, whether it's suitable for us or not and if there are any indigenous life forms that could be a threat. Remember, once Explorer 1 has landed, wherever that may be, that's it. She doesn't have the power to lift off again and be able to overcome the effect of gravity. Therefore, we have to be absolutely sure that we've made the correct decision before we land the craft that has been our home and protected us in our journey so far. The choice we will have to make will decide the future for us all."

The sound of klaxons reverberated through the engineering section, as the air was evacuated from AG Craft Bay 1, preparing it for the opening of the space door. The bay air pressure was slowly reduced until the craft was in a vacuum. Then the space door opened, allowing the AG1 craft to move out into space, its rear-facing cameras recording a comprehensive set of images of Explorer 1.

As the craft approached the planet the pilot had to reduce the sun screen over his windows, as the bright yellow light from the sun was too much for his eyes to cope with. Entering the planet's atmosphere he was able to switch over to the AG drive, saving his fuel for the climb away from the planet when he'd completed his mission.

The air increased in density as his altitude decreased, which is what he expected, although he was surprised by the buffeting experienced, as he reduced height through the collection of wispy clouds that stretched across the sky for miles. Emerging beneath the clouds, he noticed for the first time that the sky had taken on a deep pink colour. He thought that it was caused by the sun screens, which he hadn't retracted. Removing them just accentuated the colour even more. It took some time to become used to having a pink sky. He didn't like it. The sky should be blue, he thought, but beggars can't be choosers, can they?

There had been much speculation about the yellow areas on the planet's surface, so he sought out the appropriate area. When he saw the reason for the yellowing, all the theories and speculations that had been banded about on Explorer 1 couldn't have been further from the truth. The scene below him really shocked him. The yellow hue was caused by a seething mass of snake-like creatures that appeared to grow up to approximate eight feet long. The shorter ones were bright yellow and as they grew in length their colour darkened, until they took on an orange colour. Making them even more unearthly they had four long, thin spindly legs, terminating in four toes, each one bearing a long claw. They were crawling over each other, using the claws on their toes to dig into one another. When they opened their mouth to begin yet another fight, they displayed an horrendous collection of teeth, which they didn't hesitate to use on one another.

The AG craft quickly gained height in an attempt to cancel out the scene below. At this point he realised that these creatures, snakes or whatever they were, hadn't paid any attention to his presence at all which was rather unusual. (It took the pilot some months before the bad dreams about yellow snakes finally faded away.) Fortunately, the onboard cameras had recorded his encounter with the yellow snakes, so he was able to prove what he was to write in his report. Even though he was on edge following this encounter, he continued his mission, deploying various types of probes far and wide.

When the AG craft first approached the surface, a number of remote cameras were deployed to cover as much of the surface of the planet as they could, before receiving the recall signal which instructed them to stop recording and return to the craft. What marvels or horrors, depending on your point of view, they had encountered would only be revealed when their memories would be downloaded back on Explorer 1 and were made ready for all on board to see and wonder at. No doubt some of the comments would be the source of nightmares for many of them for some time to come, whereas the scientists revelled in what they saw, realising and appreciating that they were the first humans to have the privilege to study the native creatures of an alien planet.

By the time that the AG craft was safely returned to its bay on Explorer 1, information was already streaming in from the various probes that had been placed on the planet's surface. The first data shown was from the probe that dealt with atmospheric air pressure, along with the gaseous make-up of the air. As the probes were placed in their respective positions, it only took them a few seconds before they began to return their data to Explorer 1. The veritable cascade of information that was arriving on Explorer 1 was fed direfully into the comprehensive computer systems on board. As all of this data was combined together, it began to form a detailed picture of the planet below.

When the remote camera memories were being copied and combined into a presentable format, a complete picture of the planet's surface began to emerge. As one of the remote cameras was closing in on a collection of 'trees', a group of three-legged, blue furred creatures was seen scuttling into the 'trees'. One of these creatures stood its ground, attempting to drive the camera away. The self-preservation circuits within the camera performed perfectly and positioned the camera out of harm's way, moving on to another point of interest.

Those studying the indigenous creatures noticed an unusual pattern. Although there were patches of vegetation scattered all over the surface, the three-legged creatures were always in close proximity to gatherings of the yellow 'snakes'. There seemed to be some form of symbiosis between the two of them, but what form it took wasn't understood. They also didn't know what forms of life lurked in the soil, as they didn't posses any kind of burrowing probe. That was the kind of information that could only be obtained by walking on the surface and from what they'd seen, no one wanted to engage in such a foolhardy task.

As the data flowed in and was analysed, the more unsuitable for supporting human life it became and many statements and questions were uttered: "The atmosphere would be poisonous to our systems, the air pressure being twice what we're used to and on top of that the gravity's almost twice what the human frame can tolerate." "Whether any of the crops that we would need to grow would survive is debatable. What would we eat?" "What would we breathe, as we crawled about on our hands and knees?" The conclusion was rapidly reached, that this was not the home for Explorer 1, or its human cargo. The best course of action was to leave the area as soon as possible.

Bernice had been on duty for twelve hours and was sitting on her own in the refreshment area, enjoying the solitude while she drank her coffee.

"Excuse me."

Bernice looked up. It took a few seconds to unscramble her thoughts, before she replied. She saw a youngish man in the white coat of a technician and quickly scanned his nametag. "Yes, Mr Dent, how can I help you?"

"May I sit down?" he replied.

"Help yourself," said Bernice.

"I'm one of the team that's been analysing the atmospheric data and I noticed that there's a large percentage of hydrogen in the make-up of the atmosphere."

Bernice began to perk up.

"Now, I know that we're short of fuel for the propulsion engines and I wondered if we could leach some of this hydrogen for us to use as fuel." He sat still, looking at Bernice, wondering what kind of response he was about to receive.

Bernice took a long draw on her drink, as she mulled over the concept in her mind. Following a pause that seemed to last forever, she spoke. "That's a brilliant idea. It would certainly resolve our fuel dilemma. Give me twenty-four hours to think about it and you do the same. Then we can meet up in here tomorrow and compare notes. Thank you so much. A very simple solution was right in front of us and you're the only one who saw it. Well done!"

They shook hands as they parted and went their separate ways, their heads full of ideas of how to put this suggestion into practice.

That evening everyone gathered together to hear the reports about the new planet and to view the images recorded by the cameras taken down to the surface by the AG craft.

The meeting began a few minutes late to allow everyone to get settled and prepared to pay attention. The information was being presented by the pilot who took the craft down to the surface and one of the senior scientific team. The meeting began with Professor Sam M'Banu introducing a round-up of the information gathered by the various probes.

"Good evening everyone," she said and then introduced herself. "If any of you had any thoughts about settling on the planet below us, you should dismiss them immediately. I'm sorry, but the atmosphere wouldn't do you any good at all; in fact, it would kill you." She then related all the other reasons why the planet wouldn't be suitable for human habitation.

Following the professor's summary the pilot took over. "Hello everyone," he said in a broad Gallic accent, "I'm Francois Auteuil and I'm the pilot who took the AG craft down to reconnoitre. I must be honest, I didn't want to present this material to you this evening, as some of the things I saw really upset me and I'm still struggling to forget them, but it was pointed out to me that I was the best person to deal with any questions that arose from the footage. So here goes. We'll now run the sequence that the technical staff have assembled from the images collected by the various cameras."

* * *

The next morning Chris Dent received a communication from Bernice. "Had to work today. Will you please join me on the flight deck, when you're able."

Chris was rather surprised. He'd never been allowed onto the flight deck before, neither had any of his compatriots. He felt rather honoured.

A couple of hours later he knocked on the flight deck door. Following a slight pause he heard a voice, that he recognised as Bernice's, through the intercom.

"Who is it?"

"It's Chris Dent," he replied. He heard the locks release on the door and Bernice opened it to allow Chris to enter. He quickly scanned the flight deck, checking the layout. When Mike Kirkwood turned around to see who it was that Bernice had allowed to enter their domain, Chris introduced himself.

"Bernice was explaining to Ranjit and myself the idea that you had. Personally speaking, I think it's a great idea. We were looking for a complex solution whereas something straightforward was right in front of us all the time. Well done!"

"Thank you," replied a rather stunned Chris.

"Sit down here," said Bernice, pointing to a chair beside her. "I spent a great deal of time overnight, studying the propulsion engine manuals, trying to ascertain whether it was possible to modify them to run on hydrogen rather than the fuel they were designed to burn."

"Are they very different from the old type of rocket engines?" Christ enquired.

"Good question," said Bernice. "Our propulsion engines are a long way removed from the original design of the rocket engine. The principle is the same. Fuel goes in, is burnt and a big flame comes out the other end, but that's where the similarity ceases. I discussed the prospect with a couple of senior engineers last night and they feel that it's a viable challenge. They didn't think that it would be easy, although they felt confident that they would be able to do it."

"That's great news," said Chris.

"I agree," stated Mike, even though he had his back to the two of them, but he was obviously listening to their conversation. They both chuckled at Mike's intervention.

"What's next then?" asked Chris.

"I won't ask the engineers to commence any modification at the moment, until we establish from the scientific bods if gathering hydrogen from the planet's atmosphere is a viable prospect or not."

"I hope you don't expect me to approach them," asked Chris, "as I don't think that they would pay any attention to me. After all, I'm only a lowly technician and I barely feature in their circles."

"Don't put yourself down like that!" Bernice said. "Just think. You came up with the idea – they didn't, did they?"

Chris met Bernice at the entrance of the scientific and technical section and led her to the senior scientist's office. He knocked on the door, then opened it and Bernice walked in, with Chris following.

"Good afternoon," Bernice said. "I'm Bernice Heckt and this is Chris Dent."

"We are aware of Mr Dent. You can leave now Mr Dent and close the door behind you!"

Bernice turned to Chris and said, "I see what you mean." She then turned to face the scientists. "Actually, I'd like Chris to stay with us, as he was the originator of the rather clever solution to our fuel shortage situation. Do you think we could sit down?"

"Please do," came the reply.

"Thank you," she said.

"So what is it that you wish us to do then Dr Heckt?"

Bernice intended to make the most of this opportunity.

"A few days ago, Mr Dent approached me and suggested that we procure some hydrogen from the atmosphere of the planet that we're circling and use it to power the propulsion engines. I felt that the suggestion had merit. I've spent a lot of my off-duty time studying the engine manuals and have had detailed discussions with my engineers. The engines would need modification, but it would be possible to adapt them to burn hydrogen rather than their normal fuel. Would you like to take over Chris, my mouth has become very dry?"

Bernice could hear the nervousness in Chris's voice as he began to speak, although that disappeared once he got into his stride. She wanted, really, to see how well the scientists would respond to having a technician speaking authoritatively to them. She was able to determine that they didn't like having to listen, when a lowly technician spoke to them.

"...so we're here to ask you if you would be able to devise a method to extract pure hydrogen from the mixture of gases available to us. Both Dr Heckt and myself appreciate that you're somewhat limited by the restricted materials available to you, but by employing the ingenuity of those around you, it may well be possible to come up with an innovative solution."

The room was silent for a few moments as the scientists pondered over what they'd just heard, trying not to show too much enthusiasm. After all, they were the ones who usually came up with the smart ideas and they didn't want to loose face with something so critical.

"Could you both go and have a coffee for ten minutes or so while we have a discussion and when you come back we'll let you know if we're willing to go ahead with the suggestion. Then we can gather the whole department together to see what ideas there are and if we can come up with a viable plan, we'll let you know," said the scientist who seemed to be in charge.

Bernice and Chris stood up and thanked them for their time. "We'll see you in a few moments," said Bernice.

CHAPTER 29

…AND SO IT BEGINS

When Bernice and Chris returned to the scientists' office, they noticed that there had been a distinct change of attitude towards Chris. Rather than treat him in an offhand manner, as they had previously, they praised him for coming up with such a simple, but practical idea: a solution to the fuel problems that could benefit everyone on board Explorer 1.

"We'd certainly like to take up the challenge that you've placed before us and will do all that we can to achieve our goal. Dr Heckt, we'll contact you as soon as possible, although that won't be until a workable solution to the problem has been found. I hope that satisfies you both."

Chris almost fell off his chair. Not only had they been pleasant to him, they'd included him in the conversation. Out of the corner of his eye he noticed that Bernice was looking in his direction. He glanced directly at her. She smiled at him, which was her way of saying that she'd noticed his inclusion in the conversation.

Bernice turned to the scientists and said, "Thank you for your help, which will hopefully benefit all of us. We'll await your communication."

"I don't know what they had while we were away. Whatever it was it certainly changed their attitude. They even spoke nicely to me and included me in the conversation," said Chris. He just couldn't get over the way that they'd altered their attitude towards him.

"It was so obvious, wasn't it?" Bernice said in reply to Chris's musing. "I don't know who they consulted or spoke to, but whoever it was obviously put them straight and helped them to understand the importance of the project they would be part of."

Bernice hadn't appreciated that the scientists also had a superior staff member who out of view had monitored their meeting with Bernice and Chris and had told them to stop acting like petulant children and treat Chris with more respect, especially as he'd come up with such a good idea. They should forget that he was a 'lowly technician' as they called him and treat him as an equal. They weren't too keen on the idea, but they responded to the best of their ability.

While they waited for the communication from the scientific team, Bernice and Chris regularly met up for coffee and sometimes they were able to enjoy a meal together, depending on their work schedules. Chris wasn't able to reveal any information about the progress that was being made as he wasn't assigned to the team that was directly involved. That was most likely due to his lack of advanced chemical knowledge and experience of working with flammable gases such as hydrogen. It was most likely better that way, otherwise he would have felt torn between keeping information secret and informing his friend.

In a closed environment like Explorer 1, it wasn't surprising that the amount of time that Bernice and Chris spent together hadn't gone unnoticed; inevitably it was bound to happen. It did attract a few comments from time-to-time, but they didn't let it bother them. In fact, Bernice had become quite fond of Chris, but whether he realised it or not she never knew.

It was seventeen days after the meeting with the scientists that the communication from them was received by Bernice. She immediately contacted Chris who told her that he realised that something was happening, as there had been lots of toing and froing all morning, as if they were preparing for something important.

As Chris and Bernice entered scientific services they were met by one of the junior lab workers, who chatted to them as he led them to a meeting room. The three scientists that they'd met before were already in the room and they all stood up as Chris and Bernice entered.

"Come on in," one of them said and then thanked the lab worker for his help. "Sit where you like. There's fresh coffee in the corner. Please help yourselves."

They instinctively decided to sit opposite the scientists. Before Chris sat down, he asked Bernice if she would like a coffee and arranged the drinks for both of them. One they were settled, Bernice began the conversation.

"How well did you get on?" she asked. This gave the scientists the opportunity to report on their progress.

"To save me speaking all the time, I'd like to hand you over to my colleague, Dr Peter Onyemera. Peter..."

"Thank you, Ron. Well... your idea Chris gave us the most interesting challenge that we've had to deal with for some time. We actually found it very stimulating, so thank you for that. It's done us good to 'stretch' our brain cells, on this one."

Peter continued. "Anyway, I'm sure you both would like to know the outcome of all our work. I'll present it in a simplified form, as I know that neither of you are chemists. To start with we reviewed the data received from the atmospheric probe left on the planet and realised that your suggestion was going to be somewhat more straightforward than we thought. The atmosphere is mainly hydrogen, along with oxygen and a small trace of methane. The whole mixture is prevented from spontaneously combusting by the inclusion of carbon dioxide, which prevents the atmosphere igniting. To begin with we decided to remove the carbon dioxide and then try to burn the combustible gases that were left. This worked remarkably well. We feel confident that we can produce a gas that your engines will happily burn, without leaving dirty deposits in the components."

Both Bernice and Chris had smiles on their faces from hearing this excellent news.

"We'll modify one engine to start with," Bernice said, "and transfer the fuel from No. 2 engine into No. 1's tank. Next we'll clean out No. 2's tank and perform a pressure test on it to ensure that it's safe to store high-pressure gas."

"Are you sure that you'll be able to provide the volume of gas that the engines will require?" Chris asked, eager to feel part of the conversation.

"Once we've set the process running, we'll provide as much as is needed. That's so long as the AG craft can keep supplying the raw gas from the planet."

"So that's a go then," replied Bernice. "I'll get the engineers to modify No. 2 engine and perform the other work necessary ready for the first test. What a day that will be!"

As they stood up ready to leave, Chris turned to the scientists. "Thank you so much for everything you're doing. If the entire project works out as planned, Explorer 1 can get on the move again and the search for a new home can continue."

As they left scientific services they felt so much more confident than they did when they arrived, when they had been full of apprehension not knowing what the outcome would be.

"Before we have to go our separate ways, shall we go for a coffee?" suggested Bernice.

"Great idea," replied Chris.

They sat facing each other while they chatted and sipped their drinks. Bernice noticed that Chris seemed to be distracted.

"Is everything all right?" she asked.

"There's something I'd like to say, but I don't know if I should." There was a pause. "I'm going to say it anyway. Over the past few weeks, as we've spent time together, I've become very fond of you. There, I've said it!"

As Chris uttered those words, Bernice heart skipped a beat. "I've felt the same way for a while now," Bernice said in reply, "although I didn't have the nerve to say anything in case I scared you away." They sat there and looked into each other's eyes and for the first time their fingers made contact as they stretched across the table. They remained like that for a few moments, until the emotional link was broken by the sound of Chris's communicator demanding his attention.

"Sorry," he said, "I'd better answer this."

Bernice sat and watched him. Could he be the one, she thought?

Chris was ending his conversation. "Okay, I'll come and see you tomorrow morning – 'bye for now." He switched off his communicator and looked at Bernice. "Sorry about that," he said, "that's what always happens, isn't it?"

"Everything all right?" Bernice asked.

"That was my old friend Doctor McAndrew, or Doug as I always call him."

"I hope that everything's all right."

"Oh, yes. He just wants to check up on how well the bones in my ankle have knitted. If it wasn't for Doug I wouldn't have been on this trip, then we wouldn't have met. So I've a lot to thank him for."

They both realised that it was time to make a move, sadly for them in opposite directions. They stood facing each other, their fingers just touching, neither of them wanting to be the first one to move. If it hadn't been such a public place they would have kissed each other goodbye, but they'd have to save that moment for another time.

"One of us is going to have to make the first move, so ladies first," Chris said with a grin on his face.

"All right," Bernice replied, "you win this time." She half turned, kissed Chris on the cheek and then she was gone.

Chris stood there. He'd been stunned by the kiss on his cheek and didn't know what to do. He realised that people were looking at him so he decided to leave as quickly as he was able, without making a fool of himself.

Dr McAndrew was sitting at his desk, updating his patients' records, when he heard the sound of his door call. "Enter," he said, employing the electronics that didn't need him to press the door button. The door slid open and in walked Chris. "Hello Chris," Doug said, "come and take a seat."

As Chris walked across the room, Doug watched him to ascertain how well he was walking. "Any problems with the ankle?" he asked.

"No problems at all," Chris replied. "The repair job that you and your companions performed has been excellent."

"I'm pleased to hear it. Any twinges, clicks or aches?"

"No, Doc, nothing at all. It's as good as it ever was."

"Marvellous! I'd just like to scan it so that there's a visual record of the repair to become part of your records."

The scan only took a few minutes to perform and following its completion Doug asked Chris to sit down again.

"Right," he said, "that's the formal stuff over and done with, how about you then? I've heard all sorts of things about you, although I prefer to hear it first hand, from you."

Chris related his account of how he had an idea and all that had taken place following his approach to the flight engineer (Bernice) and all that had developed from there.

"Very well recounted, but you've missed out the part that both Stephen and I want to know all about. You've recently been seen in the company of a woman. We both want to know all about her. Are you willing to tell us?"

Chris, reluctantly at first, began to tell Doug all about Bernice and how well they were getting on with each other.

"That's excellent news. Stephen and I often wondered which one of the three of us would be first to have a girlfriend and you've beaten both of us. Well done. Now, the next thing is, when are we going to meet her?"

"I don't know. I haven't thought about it. It won't be for a while as the first experimental run of the modified propulsion engine is due to take place in the immediate future. So, let's get that resolved first."

"Fair enough," Doug replied. "But how about the three of us getting together for a meal?"

"That would be ideal," Chris replied. "I've missed the company of you both. You've been good friends to me and it would be great for us all to meet up again."

"I'll get it arranged," said Doug.

* * *

The first experimental run of the modified propulsion system was proposed for eight days later. That would allow enough time for engineering to complete the modifications to engine 2 and to set up the gas storage system. The scientific support team assured them that they would have been able to create enough gas for the test run(s).

Bernice and Chris didn't see much of each other during the eight-day period, as Bernice was extremely busy. When they were able to spend some time together, Bernice explained the situation to Chris.

“As you’ve probably gathered, I’m going to be quite busy over the next few weeks and we won’t have the opportunity to see each other with the frequency that we have been.”

“I understand that,” Chris interjected.

“Thanks for being so understanding,” Bernice replied. “But don’t think that I’m losing interest in you. I’ll find it as difficult as you will, so we’ll have to make the most of any time that we can snatch.”

“I’ll miss your company,” Chris said.

Bernice was sure that she could see a tear in the corner of Chris’s eyes. “I honestly believe that we’ll be stronger for this,” she said. She stood up to leave, leant across the able and kissed Chris on the lips. “I have to leave now, I’ll see you when I can.” Their fingers lightly grasped until they pulled apart as Bernice left.

As the days passed, scientific services and engineering became hives of activity neither of them wanted to have any work outstanding when the eight-day period ran out. They needn’t have worried; those involved were professionals and knew exactly what they had to do and how to achieve it.

The morning of the test run arrived. Group Captain Das appeared on the monitors to inform everyone what was due to take place that day. He told them that there was going to be a test run of one of the propulsion engines, using a different kind of fuel; one that had been created from the gases that made up the atmosphere of the planet that they were circling.

“There may well be some unusual sounds from the engine room, but don’t let that bother you. Remember, this is an experimental test, so anything could happen. If it’s successful, we could well be able to get underway once more and ultimately find our new home. Just remember there’s no need to worry. Thank you for your attention.”

When he stated that, “There’s no need to worry...” a number of those working on the project said to themselves: That shows how little you know.

The test run was due to start at midday which gave those involved the morning to make final checks and adjustments.

With half an hour to go the principal characters were all in place, having tidied themselves up following the morning's activities. It was obviously considered to be an auspicious occasion, as every engineer was wearing a clean boiler suit and all of their tools had been tidied away. Fifteen minutes to go and everywhere became silent. All of the chatter throughout the ship faded away as the clock counted down.

Bernice was on the flight deck, as you would have expected her to be, as she was the flight engineer. She controlled the engines from her panel and a two-way intercom had been installed between her position and the engineering department. It was obviously too dangerous for anyone to be outside the ship to see how the engines were functioning, so two cameras had been attached on the hull, one trained on each engine. This enabled the flight engineer and the engineers in the engine room to see how well each engine was functioning and whether any adjustments were required.

There was one minute to go...

"Thirty seconds..." announced Bernice her voice echoing throughout the ship. She reached down to the control panel and removed the safety cover from over the start pad, for engine 2.

"Fifteen seconds..." then there was a five second pause and the countdown to zero began.

The moment reached zero: Bernice pressed on the pad that should have started the engine. Nothing happened.

The chief engineer contacted the flight deck via the intercom. "Nothing happening down here."

"We'll try again. Maybe there's some air in the gas pipes."

"There couldn't be, but I suppose it's possible."

A minute later the start pad was depressed once more. This time, a spluttering was heard inside the engine. All together it took nine attempts before the engine finally fired up correctly. Once this had occurred, the engineering team were able to do some fine-tuning so that the engine was running at its peak performance.

The moment the sound of the engines, or the vibration from the engines, was either heard of felt, a huge cheer resounded from everyone onboard. The fact that one of the engines was now working correctly rekindled the possibility of locating a new home for them all. This would end their incarceration on board Explorer 1, offering the possibility to be able to walk in the open and breathe fresh air once more.

How to proceed from here was the subject of the meeting of all the department heads that was held that evening. Bernice led the meeting and proposed that engine 1 should be modified, so that maximum thrust was available to start Explorer 1 moving. Once that had been achieved the engine power could be reduced.

"What will happen to the normal rocket fuel that's already feeding engine 1?"

The chief engineer dealt with this, as it was his remit. He suggested that all of the conventional rocket fuel be pumped into a holding tank, then if ever they ran out of gas one of the engines could always be converted back to its conventional state.

Just one other question arouse that evenings: How do we replenish the gas supply? Scientific services answered this one, as they would be dealing with it first hand.

"We will, no doubt, be visiting a number of planets before we locate one that's ideal for our purposes. We'll make use of whatever atmospheric gasses we come across. We appreciate that some will be better than others, but that's the chance we have to take."

The overall conclusion was positive and the all-clear was given to go ahead with the modifications, which were completed within four days, as they knew how to go about it now.

The momentous day arrived when both engines would be tested together. Engine 1 started up more readily than engine 2 had done initially. A new sound was heard throughout Explorer 1: the reassuring, purring sound of two engines running harmoniously.

That evening there was a feast for all as they intended to pull away from their permanent position, locked between the planet and its largest moon. The biggest surprise of the evening came, after everyone had eaten. The pilot stood up and announced a special commendation was to be awarded to Chris Dent, who had come up with the idea of an alternative fuel for the propulsion engines.

"If it wasn't for him," the pilot said, "We'd have been stuck her forever. CHRIS DENT!"

Everyone clapped and applauded as a highly embarrassed Chris rose from his seat and collected his award. No one applauded more enthusiastically than Bernice, which didn't go unnoticed by her associates.

The following day, Explorer 1 pulled away from the Lagrange point, where it had been residing for the last few weeks. After using the navigation array to decide which would be the best direction to head in, Explorer 1 began its long sojourn across the galaxy, looking for a new home for its population of refugees.

~ • ~

'THE STORY CONTINUES IN PARADIGM SHIFT'